Wintry Peacock

D.H. Lawrence

ET REMOTISSIMA PROPE

Modern Voices

8-06
16⁵⁰

Modern Voices
Published by Hesperus Press Limited
4 Rickett Street, London SW6 1RU
www.hesperuspress.com

This collection first published by Hesperus Press Limited, 2006
Foreword © Amit Chaudhuri, 2006

Designed and typeset by Fraser Muggeridge studio
Printed in Jordan by National Press

ISBN: 1-84391-419-0
ISBN13: 978-1-84391-419-8

Contents

Foreword

Three of these four stories I hadn't read before, and the fourth one, 'England, my England', I'd read so long ago that it had become a memory, of a man standing, or working, in a garden, of days of sunlight and warm weather, and of something terrible happening. How these elements were related to each other wasn't clear to me any more, but my simultaneous sense of plenty and of unease with regard to the story reminded me that it had got under my skin, and there it had remained.

The reason these stories are strangely, intimately persistent is because of the very distinctive and singular way in which they approximate, and speak to, the dream-state of the embattled, ebbing human psyche in modernity. They do this in a manner quite different from surrealist art, or absurdist drama, or the allegories of Kafka, or the disjunctive collages of modernism, all of which are dependent on the idea of the subconscious or the dream as a fragmentary, associative, often 'dark' language.

For one thing, despite his un-English interest in psychoanalysis, his petulant awareness of Freud, Lawrence seems less burdened with a clear-cut theory of the subconscious than his contemporaries; he gives it no special space or location or marks in his work, but situates (as he does all else) the dissolution of self we associate with the subconscious in struggle and process – that is, at once in the narrative and in the act of composition. Lawrence will simply not adhere, even when he seems to be doing so, to the almost theological conception his contemporaries have, implicitly or explicitly, of the subconscious' relationship to 'reality': as an anterior, unbridled space beneath the social and coded fabric of life. And this means that his use of allegory and symbol – both literary gestures that are defined or renewed by some notion of the subconscious, of a concealed meaning, behind a sign, of varying degrees of complexity that needs to be uncovered – is, again, unique; which is why, perhaps, we don't often think of Lawrence these days as an allegorist or symbolist. But he is both, always exhorting us, like a preacher, through his sacred economy of signs, towards a moral awareness, and making his stories open out, through his images, into what that awareness might be like. But he's always behaving, in his stories, as if he has nothing to hide; allegory and symbol are, for him, a form of plain speaking, indivisible from instruction, directness, urgency, and sensuous immediacy. This is what gives 'England, my England', for instance, its peculiarly Lawrentian dream-like force: not dream-like in the sense of it being blurred or opaque, but like a personal intervention carried to the consciousness, Rilkean in that its directive is similar to the words the German poet imagined he heard upon viewing a ruined bust of Apollo: 'You must change your life.' But 'life' in a very different sense from Rilke's article of faith; 'life', a word that Lawrence used often, and with polemical intent, is not so much something to be changed as an augury of change itself. 'England, my England' is, thus, at once a marvellous realist tale, and an urgent parable, in which the message is part of the realism, the moral imprecation inseparable from the direct impress of the sensuous physicality that Lawrence is well known for. Lawrence, who feels himself to occupy a watershed in history, is not interested in couching his doctrine in poetry or narrative, and then disseminating it through them, as a traditional allegorist would; poetry and narrative, in Lawrence, hastily rework and improvise the allegorical mode, complicating, but never quite abandoning, its dogmatic force.

Part of the reason why the dissolution or decentring of the self that the 'subconscious' implies is not incompatible in Lawrence's work with an examination of social situations and character (the world of 'subtle human interrelationship', as he called it), is because he takes out that decentring from the individual consciousness, from Romantic 'imagination' and Proustian memory, and relocates it in the sphere of culture; specifically, in the contact with the 'other'. In this, again, Lawrence is quite unlike his contemporaries, and not of his time. The contact with the 'other' is, for Lawrence, as unsettling and renovating, and entails as radical a transformation, as the discovery of the subconscious did for the modernists. In both 'The Blind Man' and 'You Touched Me', contact (literally, the act of touching) in an inadmissible context – between man and man in the former, woman and foster-brother in the latter – leads to the simultaneous opening out of the self on to 'otherness' and an unnerving loss of identity that is characteristic of dream-states, as well as of the great cultural interfaces in history, including the colonial one.

Lawrence, strikingly, defeats our expectations of where that contact with 'otherness' should be played out, by exploring its drama in the English landscape; even, as in 'England, my England', in the English garden. The peacock in 'Wintry Peacock' is, of course, a reminder that the foreign is always at hand in England, and that there's nothing purely natural about either nature or Englishness. The opening pages of 'England, my England' took me back to Ted Hughes's poem, 'Thistles', in which nature is made uninnocent and contingent, a metaphor for the conflicted narrative of 'Englishness' rather than an eternal, unchanging resource, and the thistles seen as a 'grasped fistful / Of splintered weapons' that are thrust up from 'the underground stain of a decayed Viking. / They are like pale hair and the gutturals of dialect.'

Hughes, who owed much to Lawrence, obviously had the latter's story in mind as he was writing this: the terrible drama of the conflict between the 'old' England and the 'new' being played out in the garden of an old country house in rural England. Its first sentence finds Egbert, the husband, 'working on the edge of the common,' standing there after having 'cut the rough turf and bracken', 'straining his keen blue eyes, that had a touch of the Viking in them…' And then:

The sunlight blazed down on the earth, there was a vividness of flamy vegetation.. Strange how the savage England lingers in patches, as here, amid these shaggy gorse commons... The spirit of place lingering on, primeval, as when the Saxons came, so long ago.

This is almost sentimental, because Lawrence is entering Egbert's sensibility here, but it's also immensely compelling in the way it sets the scene; nature not as a background to the story, but a participant in the definition of meanings that the story is about. Just as Hughes compares the thistles to human features ('They are like pale hair'), Lawrence sees the couple, Egbert and Winifred, in terms of the tumultuous nature that surrounds them; 'Winifred moved with a slow grace of energy like a blossoming, red-flowered bush in motion', while Egbert was a 'born rose'. And the 'girls and the father were strong-limbed, thick-blooded people, true English, as holly trees and hawthorn are English.' As in Hughes's poem, both the difference and the relation between anthropomorphism and characterisation are broken down into living historical process, by the discovery of the 'foreign' in the native – at home, as it were – and the unnatural in the natural: the human beings, in the story, seem to move with the inevitability of states of nature, an inevitability at once tragic and renewing, while nature itself is seen in terms of the historical movements that human beings create. This, too, is the way 'Thistles' works. In Lawrence's story, dream-state and culture are immersed in one another; and the 'historical' instructs us as it cannot when we encounter it in its own domain, in the chronology of dates and developments we call 'history'.

– *Amit Chaudhuri, 2006*

Wintry Peacock

There was thin, crisp snow on the ground, the sky was blue, the wind very cold, the air clear. Farmers were just turning out the cows for an hour or so in the midday, and the smell of cowsheds was unendurable as I entered Tible. I noticed the ash twigs up in the sky were pale and luminous, passing into the blue. And then I saw the peacocks. There they were in the road before me, three of them, and tailless, brown, speckled birds, with dark blue necks and ragged crests. They stepped archly over the filigree snow, and their bodies moved with slow motion, like small, light, flat-bottomed boats. I admired them, they were curious. Then a gust of wind caught them, heeled them over as if they were three frail boats opening their feathers like ragged sails. They hopped and skipped with discomfort, to get out of the draught of the wind. And then, in the lee of the walls, they resumed their arch, wintry motion, light and unballasted now their tails were gone, indifferent. They were indifferent to my presence. I might have touched them. They turned off to the shelter of an open shed.

As I passed the end of the upper house, I saw a young woman just coming out of the back door. I had spoken to her in the summer. She recognised me at once, and waved to me. She was carrying a pail, wearing a white apron that was longer than her preposterously short skirt, and she had on the cotton bonnet. I took off my hat to her and was going on. But she put down her pail and darted with a swift, furtive movement after me.

'Do you mind waiting a minute?' she said. 'I'll be out in a minute.'

She gave me a slight, odd smile, and ran back. Her face was long and sallow and her nose rather red. But her gloomy black eyes softened caressively to me for a moment, with that momentary humility which makes a man lord of the earth.

I stood in the road, looking at the fluffy, dark red young cattle that mooed and seemed to bark at me. They seemed happy, frisky cattle, a little impudent, and either determined to go back into the warm shed, or determined not to go back, I could not decide which.

Presently the woman came forward again, her head rather ducked. But she looked up at me and smiled, with that odd, immediate intimacy, something witch-like and impossible.

'Sorry to keep you waiting,' she said. 'Shall we stand in this cart-shed – it will be more out of the wind.'

So we stood among the shafts of the open cart-shed that faced the road. Then she looked down at the ground, a little sideways, and I noticed a small black frown on her brows. She seemed to brood for a moment. Then she looked straight into my eyes, so that I blinked and wanted to turn my face aside. She was searching me for something and her look was too near. The frown was still on her keen, sallow brow.

'Can you speak French?' she asked me abruptly.

'More or less,' I replied.

'I was supposed to learn it at school,' she said. 'But I don't know a word.' She ducked her head and laughed, with a slightly ugly grimace and a rolling of her black eyes.

'No good keeping your mind full of scraps,' I answered.

But she had turned aside her sallow, long face, and did not hear what I said. Suddenly again she looked at me. She was searching. And at the same time she smiled at me, and her eyes looked softly, darkly, with infinite trustful humility into mine. I was being cajoled.

'Would you mind reading a letter for me, in French,' she said, her face immediately black and bitter-looking. She glanced at me, frowning.

'Not at all,' I said.

'It's a letter to my husband,' she said, still scrutinising.

I looked at her, and didn't quite realise. She looked too far into me; my wits were gone. She glanced round. Then she looked

4

at me shrewdly. She drew a letter from her pocket, and handed it to me. It was addressed from France to Lance-Corporal Goyte, at Tible. I took out the letter and began to read it, as mere words. '*Mon cher Alfred*' – it might have been a bit of a torn newspaper. So I followed the script: the trite phrases of a letter from a French-speaking girl to an English soldier. 'I think of you always, always. Do you think sometimes of me?' And then I vaguely realised that I was reading a man's private correspondence. And yet, how could one consider these trivial, facile French phrases private! Nothing more trite and vulgar in the world, than such a love-letter – no newspaper more obvious.

Therefore I read with a callous heart the effusions of the Belgian damsel. But then I gathered my attention. For the letter went on, '*Notre cher petit bébé* – our dear little baby was born a week ago. Almost I died, knowing you were far away, and perhaps forgetting the fruit of our perfect love. But the child comforted me. He has the smiling eyes and virile air of his English father. I pray to the Mother of Jesus to send me the dear father of my child, that I may see him with my child in his arms, and that we may be united in holy family love. Ah, my Alfred, can I tell you how I miss you, how I weep for you. My thoughts are with you always, I think of nothing but you, I live for nothing but you and our dear baby. If you do not come back to me soon, I shall die, and our child will die. But no, you cannot come back to me. But I can come to you, come to England with our child. If you do not wish to present me to your good mother and father, you can meet me in some town, some city, for I shall be so frightened to be alone in England with my child, and no one to take care of us. Yet I must come to you, I must bring my child, my little Alfred to his father, the big, beautiful Alfred that I love so much. Oh, write and tell me where I shall come. I have some money; I am not a penniless creature. I have money for myself and my dear baby –'

I read to the end. It was signed: 'Your very happy and still more unhappy Elise.' I suppose I must have been smiling.

'I can see it makes you laugh,' said Mrs Goyte, sardonically. I looked up at her.

'It's a love-letter, I know that,' she said. 'There's too many "Alfreds" in it.'

'One too many,' I said.

'Oh, yes, and what does she say – Eliza? We know her name's Eliza, that's another thing.' She grimaced a little, looking up at me with a mocking laugh.

'Where did you get this letter?' I said.

'Postman gave it me last week.'

'And is your husband at home?'

'I expect him home tonight. He's been wounded, you know, and we've been applying for him home. He was home about six weeks ago – he's been in Scotland since then. Oh, he was wounded in the leg. Yes, he's all right, a great strapping fellow. But he's lame, he limps a bit. He expects he'll get his discharge – but I don't think he will. We married? We've been married six years – and he joined up the first day of the war. Oh, he thought he'd like the life. He'd been through the South African War. No, he was sick of it, fed up. I'm living with his father and mother – I've no home of my own now. My people had a big farm – over a thousand acres – in Oxfordshire. Not like here – no. Oh, they're very good to me, his father and mother. Oh, yes, they couldn't be better. They think more of me than of their own daughters. But it's not like being in a place of your own, is it? You can't *really* do as you like. No, there's only me and his father and mother at home. Before the war? Oh, he was anything. He's had a good education – but he liked the farming better. Then he was a chauffeur. That's how he knew French. He was driving a gentleman in France for a long time –'

At this point the peacocks came round the corner on a puff of wind.

'Hello, Joey!' she called, and one of the birds came forward, on delicate legs. Its grey speckled back was very elegant, it rolled its full, dark-blue neck as it moved to her. She crouched down. 'Joey, dear,' she said, in an odd, saturnine caressive voice, 'you're bound to find me, aren't you?' She put her face forward, and the bird rolled his neck, almost touching her face with his beak, as if kissing her.

'He loves you,' I said.

She twisted her face up at me with a laugh.

'Yes,' she said, 'he loves me, Joey does,' – then, to the bird – 'and I love Joey, don't I. I *do* love Joey.' And she smoothed his feathers for a moment. Then she rose, saying, 'He's an affectionate bird.'

I smiled at the roll of her 'bir-rrd'.

'Oh, yes, he is,' she protested. 'He came with me from my home seven years ago. Those others are his descendants – but they're not like Joey – *are they, dee-urr?*' Her voice rose at the end with a witch-like cry.

Then she forgot the birds in the cart-shed and turned to business again.

'Won't you read that letter?' she said. 'Read it, so that I know what it says.'

'It's rather behind his back,' I said.

'Oh, never mind him,' she cried. 'He's been behind my back long enough – all these four years. If he never did no worse things behind my back than I do behind his, he wouldn't have cause to grumble. You read me what it says.'

Now I felt a distinct reluctance to do as she bid, and yet I began – 'My dear Alfred.'

'I guessed that much,' she said. 'Eliza's dear Alfred.' She laughed. 'How do you say it in French? *Eliza?*'

I told her, and she repeated the name with great contempt –
Elise.

'Go on,' she said. 'You're not reading.'

So I began – 'I have been thinking of you sometimes – have you been thinking of me? –'

'Of several others as well, beside her, I'll wager,' said Mrs Goyte.

'Probably not,' said I, and continued. 'A dear little baby was born here a week ago. Ah, can I tell you my feelings when I take my darling little brother into my arms –'

'I'll bet it's *his*,' cried Mrs Goyte.

'No,' I said. 'It's her mother's.'

'Don't you believe it,' she cried. 'It's a blind. You mark, it's her own right enough – and his.'

'No,' I said, 'it's her mother's.' 'He has sweet smiling eyes, but not like your beautiful English eyes –'

She suddenly struck her hand on her skirt with a wild motion, and bent down, doubled with laughter. Then she rose and covered her face with her hand.

'I'm forced to laugh at the beautiful English eyes,' she said.

'Aren't his eyes beautiful?' I asked.

'Oh, yes – *very!* Go on! *Joey, dear, dee-urr, Joey!*' – this to the peacock.

'Er – We miss you very much. We all miss you. We wish you were here to see the darling baby. Ah, Alfred, how happy we were when you stayed with us. We all loved you so much. My mother will call the baby Alfred so that we shall never forget you –'

'Of course it's his right enough,' cried Mrs Goyte.

'No,' I said. 'It's the mother's. Er – My mother is very well. My father came home yesterday – on leave. He is delighted with his son, my little brother, and wishes to have him named after you, because you were so good to us all in that terrible time, which I shall never forget. I must weep now when I think of it. Well, you are far away in England, and perhaps I shall never see you again. How did you find your dear mother and father? I am so happy that your wound is better, and that you can nearly walk –'

'How did he find his dear *wife*!' cried Mrs Goyte. 'He never told her he had one. Think of taking the poor girl in like that!'

'We are so pleased when you write to us. Yet now you are in England you will forget the family you served so well –'

'A bit too well – eh, *Joey!*' cried the wife.

'If it had not been for you we should not be alive now, to grieve and to rejoice in this life, that is so hard for us. But we have recovered some of our losses, and no longer feel the burden of poverty. The little Alfred is a great comfort to me. I hold him to my breast and think of the big, good Alfred, and I weep to think that those times of suffering were perhaps the times of a great happiness that is gone for ever.'

'Oh, but isn't it a shame, to take a poor girl in like that!' cried Mrs Goyte. 'Never to let on that he was married, and raise her hopes – I call it beastly, I do.'

'You don't know,' I said. 'You know how anxious women are to fall in love, wife or no wife. How could he help it, if she was determined to fall in love with him?'

'He could have helped it if he'd wanted.'

'Well,' I said, 'we aren't all heroes.'

'Oh, but that's different! The big, good Alfred! – did ever you hear such tommy-rot in your life! Go on – what does she say at the end?'

'Er – We shall be pleased to hear of your life in England. We all send many kind regards to your good parents. I wish you all happiness for your future days. Your very affectionate and ever-grateful Elise.'

There was silence for a moment, during which Mrs Goyte remained with her head dropped, sinister and abstracted. Suddenly she lifted her face, and her eyes flashed.

'Oh, but I call it beastly, I call it mean, to take a girl in like that.'

'Nay,' I said. 'Probably he hasn't taken her in at all. Do you think those French girls are such poor innocent things? I guess she's a great deal more downy than he.'

'Oh, he's one of the biggest fools that ever walked,' she cried.

'There you are!' said I.

'But it's his child right enough,' she said.

'I don't think so,' said I.

'I'm sure of it.'

'Oh, well,' I said, 'if you prefer to think that way.'

'What other reason has she for writing like that –'

I went out into the road and looked at the cattle.

'Who is this driving the cows?' I said. She too came out.

'It's the boy from the next farm,' she said.

'Oh, well,' said I, 'those Belgian girls! You never know where their letters will end. And, after all, it's his affair – you needn't bother.'

'Oh!' she cried, with rough scorn, 'it's not *me* that bothers. But it's the nasty meanness of it – me writing him such loving letters' – she put her hand before her face and laughed malevolently – 'and sending him parcels all the time. You bet he fed that gurrl on my parcels – I know he did. It's just like him. I'll bet they laughed together over my letters. I bet anything they did –'

'Nay,' said I. 'He'd burn your letters for fear they'd give him away.'

There was a black look on her yellow face. Suddenly a voice was heard calling. She poked her head out of the shed, and answered coolly:

'All right!' Then, turning to me: 'That's his mother looking after me.'

She laughed into my face, witch-like, and we turned down the road.

When I awoke, the morning after this episode, I found the house darkened with deep, soft snow, which had blown against the large west windows, covering them with a screen. I went outside, and saw the valley all white and ghastly below me, the trees beneath black and thin-looking like wire, the rock-faces dark between the glistening shroud, and the sky above sombre, heavy, yellowish-dark, much too heavy for this world below of hollow bluey whiteness figured with black. I felt I was in a valley of the dead. And I sensed I was a prisoner, for the snow was everywhere deep, and drifted in places. So all the morning I remained indoors, looking up the drive at the shrubs so heavily plumed with snow, at the gateposts raised high with a foot or more of extra whiteness. Or I looked down into the white-and-black valley that was utterly motionless and beyond life, a hollow sarcophagus.

Nothing stirred the whole day – no plume fell off the shrubs, the valley was as abstracted as a grove of death. I looked over at the tiny, half-buried farms away on the bare uplands beyond the valley hollow, and I thought of Tible in the snow, of the black witch-like little Mrs Goyte. And the snow seemed to lay me bare to influences I wanted to escape.

In the faint glow of the half-clear light that came about four o'clock in the afternoon, I was roused to see a motion in the snow away below, near where the thorn trees stood very black and dwarfed, like a little savage group, in the dismal white. I watched closely. Yes, there was a flapping and a struggle – a big bird, it must be, labouring in the snow. I wondered. Our biggest birds, in the valley, were the large hawks that often hung flickering opposite my windows, level with me, but high above some prey on the steep valley-side. This was much too big for a hawk – too big for any known bird. I searched in my mind for the largest English wild birds, geese, buzzards.

Still it laboured and strove, then was still, a dark spot, then struggled again. I went out of the house and down the steep slope, at risk of breaking my leg between the rocks. I knew the ground so well – and yet I got well shaken before I drew near the thorn trees.

Yes, it was a bird. It was Joey. It was the grey-brown peacock with a blue neck. He was snow-wet and spent.

'Joey – Joey, de-urr!' I said, staggering unevenly towards him. He looked so pathetic, rowing and struggling in the snow, too spent to rise, his blue neck stretching out and lying sometimes on the snow, his eye closing and opening quickly, his crest all battered.

'Joey dee-uur! Dee-urr!' I said caressingly to him. And at last he lay still, blinking, in the surged and furrowed snow, whilst I came near and touched him, stroked him, gathered him under my arm. He stretched his long, wetted neck away from me as I held him, none the less he was quiet in my arm, too tired, perhaps, to struggle. Still he held his poor, crested head away from me, and seemed sometimes to droop, to wilt, as if he might suddenly die.

He was not so heavy as I expected, yet it was a struggle to get up to the house with him again. We set him down, not too near the fire, and gently wiped him with cloths. He submitted, only now and then stretched his soft neck away from us, avoiding us helplessly. Then we set warm food by him. I *put* it to his beak, tried to make him eat. But he ignored it. He seemed to be ignorant of what we were doing, recoiled inside himself inexplicably. So we put him in a basket with cloths, and left him crouching oblivious. His food we put near him. The blinds were drawn, the house was warm, it was night. Sometimes he stirred, but mostly he huddled still, leaning his queer crested head on one side. He touched no food, and took no heed of sounds or movements. We talked of brandy or stimulants. But I realised we had best leave him alone.

In the night, however, we heard him thumping about. I got up anxiously with a candle. He had eaten some food, and scattered more, making a mess. And he was perched on the back of a heavy armchair. So I concluded he was recovered, or recovering.

The next day was clear, and the snow had frozen, so I decided to carry him back to Tible. He consented, after various flappings, to sit in a big fish-bag with his battered head peeping out with wild uneasiness. And so I set off with him, slithering down into the valley, making good progress down in the pale shadow beside the rushing waters, then climbing painfully up the arrested white valley-side, plumed with clusters of young pine trees, into the paler white radiance of the snowy, upper regions, where the wind cut fine. Joey seemed to watch all the time with wide anxious, unseeing eye, brilliant and inscrutable. As I drew near to Tible township he stirred violently in the bag, though I do not know if he had recognised the place. Then, as I came to the sheds, he looked sharply from side to side, and stretched his neck out long. I was a little afraid of him. He gave a loud, vehement yell, opening his sinister beak, and I stood still, looking at him as he struggled in the bag, shaken myself by his struggles, yet not thinking to release him.

Mrs Goyte came darting past the end of the house, her head sticking forward in sharp scrutiny. She saw me, and came forward.

'Have you got Joey?' she cried sharply, as if I were a thief.

I opened the bag, and he flopped out, flapping as if he hated the touch of the snow now. She gathered him up, and put her lips to his beak. She was flushed and handsome, her eyes bright, her hair slack, thick, but more witch-like than ever. She did not speak.

She had been followed by a grey-haired woman with a round, rather sallow face and a slightly hostile bearing.

'Did you bring him with you, then?' she asked sharply. I answered that I had rescued him the previous evening.

From the background slowly approached a slender man with a grey moustache and large patches on his trousers.

'You've got 'im back 'gain, ah see,' he said to his daughter-in-law. His wife explained how I had found Joey.

'Ah,' went on the grey man. 'It wor our Alfred scared him off, back your life. He must'a flyed ower t'valley. Tha ma' thank thy stars as 'e wor fun, Maggie. 'E'd a bin froze. They a bit nesh, you know,' he concluded to me.

'They are,' I answered. 'This isn't their country.'

'No, it isna,' replied Mr Goyte. He spoke very slowly and deliberately, quietly, as if the soft pedal were always down in his voice. He looked at his daughter-in-law as she crouched, flushed and dark, before the peacock, which would lay its long blue neck for a moment along her lap. In spite of his grey moustache and thin grey hair, the elderly man had a face young and almost delicate, like a young man's. His blue eyes twinkled with some inscrutable source of pleasure, his skin was fine and tender, his nose delicately arched. His grey hair being slightly ruffled, he had a debonair look, as of a youth who is in love.

'We mun tell 'im it's come,' he said slowly, and turning he called, 'Alfred – Alfred! Wheer's ter gotten to?'

Then he turned again to the group.

'Get up then, Maggie, lass, get up wi' thee. Tha ma'es too much o' th'bod.'

A young man approached, wearing rough khaki and knee-breeches. He was Danish-looking, broad at the loins.

'I's come back then,' said the father to the son; 'leastwise, he's bin browt back, flyed ower the Griff Low.'

The son looked at me. He had a devil-may-care bearing, his cap on one side, his hands stuck in the front pockets of his breeches. But he said nothing.

'Shall you come in a minute, master,' said the elderly woman, to me.

'Ay, come in an' ha'e a cup o' tea or summat. You'll do wi' summat, carrin' that bod. Come on, Maggie wench, let's go in.'

So we went indoors, into the rather stuffy, overcrowded living room, that was too cosy, and too warm. The son followed last, standing in the doorway. The father talked to me.

Maggie put out the teacups. The mother went into the dairy again.

'Tha'lt rouse thysen up a bit again, now, Maggie,' the father-in-law said – and then to me: ''ers not bin very bright sin' Alfred came whoam, an' the bod flyed awee. 'E come whoam a Wednesday night, Alfred did. But ay, you knowed, didna yer. Ay, 'e comed 'a Wednesday – an' I reckon there wor a bit of a to-do between 'em, worn't there, Maggie?'

He twinkled maliciously to his daughter-in-law, who was flushed, brilliant and handsome.

'Oh, be quiet, Father. You're wound up, by the sound of you,' she said to him, as if crossly. But she could never be cross with him.

''Ers got 'er colour back this mornin',' continued the father-in-law slowly. 'It's bin heavy weather wi' 'er this last two days. Ay – 'er's bin northeast sin 'er seed you a Wednesday.'

'Father, do stop talking. You'd wear the leg off an iron pot. I can't think where you've found your tongue, all of a sudden,' said Maggie, with caressive sharpness.

'Ah've found it wheer I lost it. Aren't goin' ter come in an' sit thee down, Alfred?'

But Alfred turned and disappeared.

''E's got th' monkey on 'is back ower this letter job,' said the father secretly to me. 'Mother, 'er knows nowt about it. Lot o' tom-foolery, isn't it? Ay! What's good o' makkin' a peck o' trouble over what's far enough off, an' ned niver come no nigher. No – not a smite o' use. That's what I tell 'er. 'Er should ta'e no notice on't. Ty, what can y' expect.'

The mother came in again, and the talk became general. Maggie flashed her eyes at me from time to time, complacent and satisfied, moving among the men. I paid her little compliments, which she did not seem to hear. She attended to me with a kind of sinister, witch-like graciousness, her dark head ducked between her shoulders, at once humble and powerful. She was happy as a child attending to her father-in-law and to me. But there was something ominous between her eyebrows, as if a dark moth were settled there – and something ominous in her bent, hulking bearing.

She sat on a low stool by the fire, near her father-in-law. Her head was dropped, she seemed in a state of abstraction. From time to time she would suddenly recover, and look up at us, laughing and chatting. Then she would forget again. Yet in her hulked black forgetting she seemed very near to us.

The door having been opened, the peacock came slowly in, prancing calmly. He went near to her and crouched down, coiling his blue neck. She glanced at him, but almost as if she did not observe him. The bird sat silent, seeming to sleep, and the woman also sat hulked and silent, seemingly oblivious. Then once more there was a heavy step, and Alfred entered. He looked at his wife, and he looked at the peacock crouching by her. He stood large in the doorway, his hands stuck in front of him, in his breeches pockets. Nobody spoke. He turned on his heel and went out again.

I rose also to go. Maggie started as if coming to herself.

'Must you go?' she asked, rising and coming near to me, standing in front of me, twisting her head sideways and looking up at me. 'Can't you stop a bit longer? We can all be cosy today, there's nothing to do outdoors.' And she laughed, showing her teeth oddly. She had a long chin.

I said I must go. The peacock uncoiled and coiled again his long blue neck, as he lay on the hearth. Maggie still stood close in front of me, so that I was acutely aware of my waistcoat buttons.

'Oh, well,' she said, 'you'll come again, won't you? Do come again.'

I promised.

'Come to tea one day – yes, do!'

I promised – one day.

The moment I went out of her presence I ceased utterly to exist for her – as utterly as I ceased to exist for Joey. With her curious abstractedness she forgot me again immediately. I knew it as I left her. Yet she seemed almost in physical contact with me while I was with her.

The sky was all pallid again, yellowish. When I went out there was no sun; the snow was blue and cold. I hurried away down the hill, musing on Maggie. The road made a loop down the sharp face of the slope. As I went crunching over the laborious snow I became aware of a figure striding down the steep scarp to intercept me. It was a man with his hands in front of him, half stuck in his breeches pockets, and his shoulders square – a real farmer of the hills; Alfred, of course. He waited for me by the stone fence.

'Excuse me,' he said as I came up.

I came to a halt in front of him and looked into his sullen blue eyes. He had a certain odd haughtiness on his brows. But his blue eyes stared insolently at me.

'Do you know anything about a letter – in French – that my wife opened – a letter of mine?'

'Yes,' said I. 'She asked me to read it to her.'

He looked square at me. He did not know exactly how to feel.

'What was there in it?' he asked.

'Why?' I said. 'Don't you know?'

'She makes out she's burnt it,' he said.

'Without showing it you?' I asked.

He nodded slightly. He seemed to be meditating as to what line of action he should take. He wanted to know the contents of the letter – he must know – and therefore he must ask me, for evidently his wife had taunted him. At the same time, no doubt, he would like to wreak untold vengeance on my unfortunate person. So he eyed me, and I eyed him, and neither of us spoke. He did not want to repeat his request to me. And yet I only looked at him, and considered.

Suddenly he threw back his head and glanced down the valley. Then he changed his position – he was a horse-soldier. Then he looked at me confidentially.

'She burnt the blasted thing before I saw it,' he said.

'Well,' I answered slowly, 'she doesn't know herself what was in it.'

He continued to watch me narrowly. I grinned to myself.

'I didn't like to read her out what there was in it,' I continued.

He suddenly flushed so that the veins in his neck stood out, and he stirred again uncomfortably.

'The Belgian girl said her baby had been born a week ago, and that they were going to call it Alfred,' I told him.

He met my eyes. I was grinning. He began to grin, too.

'Good luck to her,' he said.

'Best of luck,' said I.

'And what did you tell *her*?' he asked.

'That the baby belonged to the old mother – that it was brother to your girl, who was writing to you as a friend of the family.'

He stood smiling, with the long, subtle malice of a farmer.

'And did she take it in?' he asked.

'As much as she took anything else.'

He stood grinning fixedly. Then he broke into a short laugh.

'Good for *her*,' he exclaimed cryptically.

And then he laughed aloud once more, evidently feeling he had won a big move in his contest with his wife.

'What about the other woman?' I asked.

'Who?'

'Elise.'

'Oh' – he shifted uneasily – 'she was all right –'

'You'll be getting back to her,' I said.

He looked at me. Then he made a grimace with his mouth.

'Not me,' he said. 'Back your life it's a plant.'

'You don't think the *cher petit bébé* is a little Alfred?'

'It might be,' he said.

'Only might?'

'Yes – an' there's lots of mites in a pound of cheese.' He laughed boisterously but uneasily. 'What did she say, exactly?' he asked.

I began to repeat, as well as I could, the phrases of the letter:

' "*Mon cher Alfred – figure-toi comme je suis desolée –*"¹'

He listened with some confusion. When I had finished all I could remember, he said, 'They know how to pitch you out a letter, those Belgian lasses.'

'Practice,' said I.

'They get plenty,' he said.

There was a pause.

'Oh, well,' he said. 'I've never got that letter, anyhow.'

The wind blew fine and keen, in the sunshine, across the snow. I blew my nose and prepared to depart.

'And *she* doesn't know anything?' he continued, jerking his head up the hill in the direction of Tible.

'She knows nothing but what I've said – that is, if she really burnt the letter.'

'I believe she burnt it,' he said, 'for spite. She's a little devil, she is. But I shall have it out with her.' His jaw was stubborn and sullen. Then suddenly he turned to me with a new note.

'Why?' he said. 'Why didn't you wring that b*** peacock's neck – that b*** Joey?'

'Why?' I said. 'What for?'

'I hate the brute,' he said. 'I had a shot at him –'

I laughed. He stood and mused.

'Poor little Elise,' he murmured.

'Was she small – *petite*?' I asked. He jerked up his head.

'No,' he said. 'Rather tall.'

'Taller than your wife, I suppose.'

Again he looked into my eyes. And then once more he went into a loud burst of laughter that made the still, snow-deserted valley clap again.

'God, it's a knockout!' he said, thoroughly amused. Then he stood at ease, one foot out, his hands in his breeches pockets, in front of him, his head thrown back, a handsome figure of a man.

'But I'll do that blasted Joey in –' he mused.

I ran down the hill, shouting with laughter.

England, My England

He was working on the edge of the common, beyond the small brook that ran in the dip at the bottom of the garden, carrying the garden path in continuation from the plank bridge on to the common. He had cut the rough turf and bracken, leaving the grey, dryish soil bare. But he was worried because he could not get the path straight; there was a pleat between his brows. He had set up his sticks, and taken the sights between the big pine trees, but for some reason everything seemed wrong. He looked again, straining his keen blue eyes, that had a touch of the Viking in them, through the shadowy pine trees as through a doorway, at the green-grassed garden path rising from the shadow of alders by the log bridge up to the sunlit flowers. Tall white and purple columbines, and the butt-end of the old Hampshire cottage that crouched near the earth amid flowers, blossoming in the bit of shaggy wildness round about.

There was a sound of children's voices calling and talking: high, childish, girlish voices, slightly didactic and tinged with domineering: 'If you don't come quick, nurse, I shall run out there to where there are snakes.' And nobody had the sangfroid to reply: 'Run then, little fool.' It was always, 'No, darling. Very well, darling. In a moment, darling. Darling, you *must* be patient.'

His heart was hard with disillusion: a continual gnawing and resistance. But he worked on. What was there to do but submit!

The sunlight blazed down upon the earth, there was a vividness of flamy vegetation, of fierce seclusion amid the savage peace of the commons. Strange how the savage England lingers in patches, as here, amid these shaggy gorse commons, and marshy, snake-infested places near the foot of the South Downs. The spirit of place lingering on, primeval, as when the Saxons came, so long ago.

Ah, how he had loved it! The green garden path, the tufts of flowers, purple and white columbines, and great oriental red poppies with their black chaps and mulleins tall and yellow, this flamy garden which had been a garden for a thousand years, scooped out in the little hollow among the snake-infested commons. He had made it flame with flowers, in a sun cup under its hedges and trees. So old, so old a place! And yet he had re-created it.

The timbered cottage with its sloping, cloak-like roof was old and forgotten. It belonged to the old England of hamlets and yeomen. Lost all alone on the edge of the common, at the end of a wide, grassy, briar-entangled lane shaded with oak, it had never known the world of today. Not till Egbert came with his bride. And he had come to fill it with flowers.

The house was ancient and very uncomfortable. But he did not want to alter it. Ah, marvellous to sit there in the wide, black, time-old chimney, at night when the wind roared overhead, and the wood which he had chopped himself sputtered on the hearth! Himself on one side of the angle, and Winifred on the other.

Ah, how he had wanted her: Winifred! She was young and beautiful and strong with life, like a flame in sunshine. She moved with a slow grace of energy like a blossoming, red-flowered bush in motion. She, too, seemed to come out of the old England, ruddy, strong, with a certain crude, passionate quiescence and a hawthorn robustness. And he, he was tall and slim and agile, like an English archer with his long supple legs and fine movements. Her hair was nut-brown and all in energic curls and tendrils. Her eyes were nut-brown, too, like a robin's for brightness. And he was white-skinned with fine, silky hair that had darkened from fair, and a slightly arched nose of an old country family. They were a beautiful couple.

The house was Winifred's. Her father was a man of energy, too. He had come from the north poor. Now he was moderately rich. He had bought this fair stretch of inexpensive land, down in Hampshire. Not far from the tiny church of the almost extinct hamlet stood his own house, a commodious old farmhouse standing back from the road across a bare grassed yard. On one side of this quadrangle was the long, long barn or shed which he had made into a cottage for his youngest daughter Priscilla. One saw little blue-and-white check curtains at the long windows, and inside, overhead, the grand old timbers of the high-pitched shed. This was Prissy's house. Fifty yards away was the pretty little new cottage which he had built for his daughter Magdalen, with the vegetable garden stretching away to the oak copse. And then away beyond the lawns and rose trees of the house-garden went the track across a shaggy, wild grass space, towards the ridge of tall black pines that grew on a dyke bank, through the pines and above the sloping little bog, under the wide, desolate oak trees, till there was Winifred's cottage crouching unexpectedly in front, so much alone, and so primitive.

It was Winifred's own house, and the gardens and the bit of common and the boggy slope were hers: her tiny domain. She had married just at the time when her father had bought the estate, about ten years before the war, so she had been able to come to Egbert with this for a marriage portion. And who was more delighted, he or she, it would be hard to say. She was only twenty at the time, and he was only twenty-one. He had about a hundred and fifty pounds a year of his own – and nothing else but his very considerable personal attractions. He had no profession; he earned nothing. But he talked of literature and music, he had a passion for old folk music, collecting folk-songs and folk-dances, studying the morris dance and the old customs. Of course in time he would make money in these ways.

Meanwhile youth and health and passion and promise. Winifred's father was always generous, but still, he was a man from the north with a hard head and a hard skin too, having received a good many knocks. At home he kept the hard head out of sight, and played at poetry and romance with his literary wife and his sturdy, passionate girls. He was a man of courage, not given to complaining, bearing his burdens by himself. No, he did not let the world intrude far into his home. He had a delicate, sensitive wife whose poetry won some fame in the narrow world of letters. He himself, with his tough old barbarian fighting spirit, had an almost childlike delight in verse, in sweet poetry and in the delightful game of a cultured home. His blood was strong even to coarseness. But that only made the home more vigorous, more robust and Christmassy. There was always a touch of Christmas about him, now he was well off. If there was poetry after dinner, there were also chocolates and nuts, and good little out-of-the-way things to be munching.

Well then, into this family came Egbert. He was made of quite a different paste. The girls and the father were strong-limbed, thick-blooded people, true English, as holly trees and hawthorn are English. Their culture was grafted on to them, as one might perhaps graft a common pink rose onto a thornstem. It flowered oddly enough, but it did not alter their blood.

And Egbert was a born rose. The age-long breeding had left him with a delightful spontaneous passion. He was not clever, nor even 'literary'. No, but the intonation of his voice, and the movement of his supple, handsome body, and the fine texture of his flesh and his hair, the slight arch of his nose, the quickness of his blue eyes would easily take the place of poetry. Winifred loved him, loved him, this southerner, as a higher being. A *higher* being, mind you. Not a deeper. And as for him, he loved her in passion with every fibre of him. She was the very warm stuff of life to him.

Wonderful then, those days at Crockham Cottage, the first days, all alone save for the woman who came to work in the mornings. Marvellous days, when she had all his tall, supple, fine-fleshed youth to herself, for herself, and he had her like a ruddy fire into which he could cast himself for rejuvenation. Ah, that it might never end, this passion, this marriage! The flame of their two bodies burnt again into that old cottage, that was haunted already by so much bygone, physical desire. You could not be in the dark room for an hour without the influences coming over you. The hot blood-desire of bygone yeomen, there in this old den where they had lusted and bred for so many generations. The silent house, dark, with thick, timbered walls and the big black chimney-place, and the sense of secrecy. Dark, with low, little windows, sunk into the earth. Dark, like a lair where strong beasts had lurked and mated, lonely at night and lonely by day, left to themselves and their own intensity for so many generations. It seemed to cast a spell on the two young people. They became different. There was a curious secret glow about them, a certain slumbering flame, hard to understand, that enveloped them both. They too felt that they did not belong to the London world any more. Crockham had changed their blood: the sense of the snakes that lived and slept even in their own garden, in the sun, so that he, going forward with the spade, would see a curious coiled brownish pile on the black soil, which suddenly would start up, hiss, and dazzle rapidly away, hissing. One day Winifred heard the strangest scream from the flower-bed under the low window of the living room, ah, the strangest scream, like the very soul of the dark past crying aloud. She ran out, and saw a long brown snake on the flower-bed, and in its flat mouth the one hind leg of a frog was striving to escape, and screaming its strange, tiny, bellowing scream. She looked at the snake, and from its sullen flat head it looked at her, obstinately. She gave a cry, and it released the frog and slid angrily away.

That was Crockham. The spear of modern invention had not passed through it, and it lay there secret, primitive, savage

27

as when the Saxons first came. And Egbert and she were caught there, caught out of the world.

He was not idle, nor was she. There were plenty of things to be done, the house to be put into final repair after the workmen had gone, cushions and curtains to sew, the paths to make, the water to fetch and attend to, and then the slope of the deep-soiled, neglected garden to level, to terrace with little terraces and paths, and to fill with flowers. He worked away, in his shirt-sleeves, worked all day intermittently doing this thing and the other. And she, quiet and rich in herself, seeing him stooping and labouring away by himself, would come to help him, to be near him. He of course was an amateur – a born amateur. He worked so hard, and did so little, and nothing he ever did would hold together for long. If he terraced the garden, he held up the earth with a couple of long narrow planks that soon began to bend with the pressure from behind, and would not need many years to rot through and break and let the soil slither all down again in a heap towards the stream-bed. But there you are. He had not been brought up to come to grips with anything, and he thought it would do. Nay, he did not think there was anything else except little temporary contrivances possible, he who had such a passion for his old enduring cottage, and for the old enduring things of the bygone England. Curious that the sense of permanency in the past had such a hold over him, whilst in the present he was all amateurish and sketchy.

Winifred could not criticise him. Town-bred, everything seemed to her splendid, and the very digging and shovelling itself seemed romantic. But neither Egbert nor she yet realised the difference between work and romance.

Godfrey Marshall, her father, was at first perfectly pleased with the ménage down at Crockham Cottage. He thought Egbert was wonderful, the many things he accomplished, and he was gratified by the glow of physical passion between the two young people. To the man who in London still worked hard to keep steady his modest fortune, the thought of this young couple digging away and loving one another down at Crockham Cottage, buried deep among the commons and marshes, near the pale-showing bulk of the downs, was like a chapter of living romance. And they drew the sustenance for their fire of passion from him, from the old man. It was he who fed their flame. He triumphed secretly in the thought. And it was to her father that Winifred still turned, as the one source of all surety and life and support. She loved Egbert with passion. But behind her was the power of her father. It was the power of her father she referred to, whenever she needed to refer. It never occurred to her to refer to Egbert, if she were in difficulty or doubt. No, in all the *serious* matters she depended on her father.

For Egbert had no intention of coming to grips with life. He had no ambition whatsoever. He came from a decent family, from a pleasant country home, from delightful surroundings. He should, of course, have had a profession. He should have studied law or entered business in some way. But no – that fatal three pounds a week would keep him from starving as long as he lived, and he did not want to give himself into bondage. It was not that he was idle. He was always doing something, in his amateurish way. But he had no desire to give himself to the world, and still less had he any desire to fight his way in the world. No, no, the world wasn't worth it. He wanted to ignore it, to go his own way apart, like a casual pilgrim down the forsaken sidetracks. He loved his wife, his cottage and garden. He would make his life there, as a sort of epicurean hermit. He loved the past, the old music and dances and customs of old England. He would try and live in the spirit of these, not in the spirit of the world of business.

But often Winifred's father called her to London, for he loved to have his children round him. So Egbert and she must have a tiny flat in town, and the young couple must transfer themselves from time to time from the country to the city. In town Egbert had plenty of friends, of the same ineffectual sort as himself, tampering with the arts, literature, painting, sculpture, music. He was not bored.

Three pounds a week, however, would not pay for all this. Winifred's father paid. He liked paying. He made her only a very small allowance, but he often gave her ten pounds – or gave Egbert ten pounds. So they both looked on the old man as the mainstay. Egbert didn't mind being patronised and paid for. Only when he felt the family was a little *too* condescending, on account of money, he began to get huffy.

Then of course children came: a lovely little blonde daughter with a head of thistledown. Everybody adored the child. It was the first exquisite blonde thing that had come into the family, a little mite with the white, slim, beautiful limbs of its father, and as it grew up the dancing, dainty movement of a wild little daisy spirit. No wonder the Marshalls all loved the child; they called her Joyce. They themselves had their own grace, but it was slow, rather heavy. They had every one of them strong, heavy limbs and darkish skins, and they were short in stature. And now they had for one of their own this light little cowslip child. She was like a little poem in herself.

But nevertheless, she brought a new difficulty. Winifred must have a nurse for her. Yes, yes, there must be a nurse. It was the family decree. Who was to pay for the nurse? The grandfather – seeing the father himself earned no money. Yes, the grandfather would pay, as he had paid all the lying-in expenses. There came a slight sense of money-strain. Egbert was living on his father-in-law.

After the child was born, it was never quite the same between him and Winifred. The difference was at first hardly perceptible. But it was there. In the first place Winifred had a new centre of interest. She was not going to adore her child. But she had what the modern mother so often has in the place of spontaneous love: a profound sense of duty towards her child. Winifred appreciated her darling little girl, and felt a deep sense of duty towards her. Strange, that this sense of duty should go deeper than the love for her husband. But so it was. And so it often is. The responsibility of motherhood was the prime responsibility in Winifred's heart; the responsibility of wifehood came a long way second.

Her child seemed to link her up again in a circuit with her own family. Her father and mother, herself, and her child, that was the human trinity for her. Her husband? Yes, she loved him still. But that was like play. She had an almost barbaric sense of duty and of family. Till she married, her first human duty had been towards her father: he was the pillar, the source of life, the everlasting support. Now another link was added to the chain of duty: her father, herself and her child.

Egbert was out of it. Without anything happening, he was gradually, unconsciously excluded from the circle. His wife still loved him, physically. But, but – he was *almost* the unnecessary party in the affair. He could not complain of Winifred. She still did her duty towards him. She still had a physical passion for him, that physical passion on which he had put all his life and soul. But – but –

It was for a long while an ever-recurring *but*. And then, after the second child, another blonde, winsome touching little thing, not so proud and flamelike as Joyce – after Annabel came, then Egbert began truly to realise how it was. His wife still loved him. But – and now the but had grown enormous – her physical love for him was of secondary importance to her. It became ever less important. After all, she had had it, this physical passion, for two years now. It was not this that one lived from. No, no – something sterner, realer.

She began to resent her own passion for Egbert – just a little she began to despise it. For after all there he was, he was charming, he was lovable, he was terribly desirable. But – but – oh, the awful looming cloud of that *but!* – he did not stand firm in the landscape of her life like a tower of strength, like a great pillar of significance. No, he was like a cat one has about the house, which will one day disappear and leave no trace. He was like a flower in the garden, trembling in the wind of life, and then gone, leaving nothing to show. As an adjunct, as an accessory, he was perfect. Many a woman would have adored to have him about her all her life, the most beautiful and desirable of all her possessions. But Winifred belonged to another school.

The years went by, and instead of coming more to grips with life, he relaxed more. He was of a subtle, sensitive, passionate nature. But he simply *would* not give himself to what Winifred called life, *Work*. No, he would not go into the world and work for money. No, he just would not. If Winifred liked to live beyond their small income – well, it was her lookout.

And Winifred did not really want him to go out into the world to work for money. Money became, alas, a word like a firebrand between them, setting them both aflame with anger. But that is because we must talk in symbols. Winifred did not really care about money. She did not care whether he earned or did not earn anything. Only she knew she was dependent on her father for three-fourths of the money spent for herself and her children, that she let that be the *casus belli*, the drawn weapon between herself and Egbert.

What did she want – what did she want? Her mother once said to her, with that characteristic touch of irony, 'Well, dear, if it is your fate to consider the lilies, that toil not, neither do they spin, that is one destiny among many others, and perhaps not so unpleasant as most. Why do you take it amiss, my child?'

The mother was subtler than her children, they very rarely knew how to answer her. So Winifred was only more confused. It was not a question of lilies. At least, if it were a question of lilies, then her children were the little blossoms. They at least *grew*. Doesn't Jesus say, 'Consider the lilies *how they grow*'? Good then, she had her growing babies. But as for that other tall, handsome flower of a father of theirs, he was full grown already, so she did not want to spend her life considering him in the flower of his days.

No, it was not that he didn't earn money. It was not that he was idle. He was *not* idle. He was always doing something, always working away, down at Crockham, doing little jobs. But, oh dear, the little jobs – the garden paths – the gorgeous flowers – the chairs to mend, old chairs to mend!

It was that he stood for nothing. If he had done something unsuccessfully, and *lost* what money they had! If he had but striven with something. Nay, even if he had been wicked, a waster, she would have been more free. She would have had something to resist, at least. A waster stands for something, really. He says, 'No, I will not aid and abet society in this business of increase and hanging together, I will upset the apple-cart as much as I can, in my small way.' Or else he says, 'No, I will *not* bother about others. If I have lusts, they are my own, and I prefer them to other people's virtues.' So, a waster, a scamp, takes a sort of stand. He exposes himself to opposition and final castigation, at any rate in story-books.

But Egbert! What are you to do with a man like Egbert? He had no vices. He was really kind, nay generous. And he was not weak. If he had been weak Winifred could have been kind to him. But he did not even give her that consolation. He was not weak, and he did not want her consolation or her kindness. No, thank you. He was of a fine passionate temper, and of a rarer steel than she. He knew it, and she knew it. Hence she was only the more baffled and maddened, poor thing. He, the higher, the finer, in his way the stronger, played with his garden, and his old folk-songs and morris dances, just played, and let her support the pillars of the future on her own heart.

And he began to get bitter, and a wicked look began to come on his face. He did not give in to her, not he. There were seven devils inside his long, slim, white body. He was healthy, full of restrained life. Yes, even he himself had to lock up his own vivid life inside himself, now she would not take it from him. Or rather, now that she only took it occasionally. For she had to yield at times. She loved him so, she desired him so, he was so exquisite to her, the fine creature that he was, finer than herself. Yes, with a groan she had to give in to her own unquenched passion for him. And he came to her then – ah, terrible, ah, wonderful; sometimes she wondered how either of them could live after the terror of the passion that swept between them. It was to her as if pure lightning, flash after flash, went through every fibre of her, till extinction came.

But it is the fate of human beings to live on. And it is the fate of clouds that seem nothing but bits of vapour slowly to pile up, to pile up and fill the heavens and blacken the sun entirely.

So it was. The love came back, the lightning of passion flashed tremendously between them. And there was blue sky and gorgeousness for a little while. And then, as inevitably, as inevitably, slowly the clouds began to edge up again above the horizon, slowly, slowly to lurk about the heavens, throwing an occasional cold and hateful shadow, slowly, slowly to congregate, to fill the empyrean space.

And as the years passed, the lightning cleared the sky more and more rarely, less and less the blue showed. Gradually the grey lid sank down upon them, as if it would be permanent.

Why didn't Egbert do something, then? Why didn't he come to grips with life? Why wasn't he like Winifred's father, a pillar of society, even if a slender, exquisite column? Why didn't he go into harness of some sort? Why didn't he take *some* direction?

Well, you can bring an ass to the water, but you cannot make him drink. The world was the water and Egbert was the ass. And he wasn't having any. He couldn't, he just couldn't. Since necessity did not force him to work for his bread and butter, he would not work for work's sake. You can't make the columbine flowers nod in January, nor make the cuckoo sing in England at Christmas. Why? It isn't his season. He doesn't want to. Nay, he *can't* want to.

And there it was with Egbert. He couldn't link up with the world's work, because the basic desire was absent from him. Nay, at the bottom of him he had an even stronger desire: to hold aloof. To hold aloof. To do nobody any damage. But to hold aloof. It was not his season.

Perhaps he should not have married and had children. But you can't stop the waters flowing. Which held true for Winifred, too. She was not made to endure aloof. Her family tree was a robust vegetation that had to be stirring and believing. In one direction or another her life *had* to go. In her own home she had known nothing of this diffidence which she found in Egbert, and which she could not understand, and which threw her into such dismay. What was she to do, what was she to do, in face of this terrible diffidence?

It was all so different in her own home. Her father may have had his own misgivings, but he kept them to himself. Perhaps he had no very profound belief in this world of ours, this society that we have elaborated with so much effort, only to find ourselves elaborated to death at last. But Godfrey Marshall was of tough, rough fibre, not without a vein of healthy cunning through it all. It was for him a question of winning through, and leaving the rest to heaven. Without having many illusions to grace him, he still *did* believe in heaven. In a dark and unquestioning way, he had a sort of faith: an acrid faith like the sap of some not-to-be-exterminated tree. Just a blind acrid faith as sap is blind and acrid, and yet pushes on in growth and in faith. Perhaps he was unscrupulous, but only as a striving tree is unscrupulous, pushing its single way in a jungle of others.

In the end, it is only this robust, sap-like faith that keeps man going. He may live on for many generations inside the shelter of the social establishment that he has erected for himself, as pear trees and currant bushes would go on bearing fruit for many seasons, inside a walled garden, even if the race of man were suddenly exterminated. But bit by bit the wall-fruit-trees would gradually pull down the very walls that sustained them. Bit by bit every establishment collapses, unless it is renewed or restored by living hands, all the while.

Egbert could not bring himself to any more of this restoring or renewing business. He was not aware of the fact, but awareness doesn't help much anyhow. He just couldn't. He had the stoic and epicurean quality of his old, fine breeding. His father-in-law, however, though he was not one bit more of a fool than Egbert, realised that since we are here we may as well live. And so he applied himself to his own tiny section of the social work, and to doing the best for his family, and to leaving the rest to the ultimate will of heaven. A certain robustness of blood made him able to go on. But sometimes even from him spurted a sudden gall of bitterness against the world and its make-up. And yet – he had his own will to succeed, and this carried him through. He refused to ask himself what the success would amount to. It amounted to the estate down in Hampshire, and his children lacking for nothing, and himself of some importance in the world: and *basta! – Basta! Basta!*[2]

Nevertheless do not let us imagine that he was a common pusher. He was not. He knew as well as Egbert what disillusion meant. Perhaps in his soul he had the same estimation of success. But he had a certain acrid courage, and a certain will to power. In his own small circle he would emanate power, the single power of his own blind self. With all his spoiling of his children, he was still the father of the old English type. He was too wise to make laws and to domineer in the abstract. But he had kept, and all honour to him, a certain primitive dominion over the souls of his children, the old, almost magic prestige of paternity. There it was, still burning in him, the old smoky torch or paternal godhead.

And in the sacred glare of this torch his children had been brought up. He had given the girls every liberty, at last. But he had never really let them go beyond his power. And they, venturing out into the hard white light of our fatherless world, learnt to see with the eyes of the world. They learnt to criticise their father, even, from some effulgence of worldly white light, to see him as inferior. But this was all very well in the head. The moment they forgot their tricks of criticism, the old red glow of his authority came over them again. He was not to be quenched.

Let the psychoanalyst talk about father complex. It is just a word invented. Here was a man who had kept alive the old red flame of fatherhood, fatherhood that had even the right to sacrifice the child to God, like Isaac. Fatherhood that had life-and-death authority over the children: a great natural power. And till his children could be brought under some other great authority as girls, or could arrive at manhood and become themselves centres of the same power, continuing the same male mystery as men, until such time, willy-nilly, Godfrey Marshall would keep his children.

It had seemed as if he might lose Winifred. Winifred had *adored* her husband, and looked up to him as to something wonderful. Perhaps she had expected in him another great authority, a male authority greater, finer than her father's. For having once known the glow of male power, she would not easily turn to the cold white light of feminine independence. She would hunger, hunger all her life for the warmth and shelter of true male strength.

And hunger she might, for Egbert's power lay in the abnegation of power. He was himself the living negative of power. Even of responsibility. For the negation of power at last means the negation of responsibility. As far as these things went, he would confine himself to himself. He would try to confine his own *influence* even to himself. He would try, as far as possible, to abstain from influencing his children by assuming any responsibility for them. 'A little child shall lead them –' his child should lead, then. He would try not to make it go in any direction whatever. He would abstain from influencing it. Liberty! –

Poor Winifred was like a fish out of water in this liberty, gasping for the denser element which should contain her. Till her child came. And then she knew that she must be responsible for it, that she must have authority over it.

But here Egbert silently and negatively stepped in. Silently, negatively, but fatally he neutralised her authority over her children.

There was a third little girl born. And after this Winifred wanted no more children. Her soul was turning to salt.

So she had charge of the children, they were her responsibility. The money for them had come from her father. She would do her very best for them, and have command over their life and death. But no! Egbert would not take the responsibility. He would not even provide the money. But he would not let her have her way. Her dark, silent, passionate authority he would not allow. It was a battle between them, the battle between liberty and the old blood-power. And of course he won. The little girls loved him and adored him. 'Daddy! Daddy!' They could do as they liked with him. Their mother would have ruled them. She would have ruled them passionately, with indulgence, with the old dark magic of parental authority, something looming and unquestioned and, after all, divine – if we believe in divine authority. The Marshalls did, being Catholic.

And Egbert, he turned her old dark, Catholic blood-authority into a sort of tyranny. He would not leave her her children. He stole them from her, and yet without assuming responsibility for them. He stole them from her, in emotion and spirit, and left her only to command their behaviour. A thankless lot for a mother. And her children adored him, adored him, little knowing the empty bitterness they were preparing for themselves when they too grew up to have husbands: husbands such as Egbert, adorable and null.

Joyce, the eldest, was still his favourite. She was now a quicksilver little thing of six years old. Barbara, the youngest, was a toddler of two years. They spent most of their time down at Crockham, because he wanted to be there. And even Winifred loved the place really. But now, in her frustrated and blinded state, it was full of menace for her children. The adders, the poison-berries, the brook, the marsh, the water that might not be pure – one thing and another. From mother and nurse it was a guerilla gunfire of commands, and blithe, quicksilver disobedience from the three blonde, never-still little girls. Behind the girls was the father, against mother and nurse. And so it was.

'If you don't come quick, nurse, I shall run out there to where there are snakes.'

'Joyce, you *must* be patient. I'm just changing Annabel.'

There you are. There it was, always the same. Working away on the common across the brook he heard it. And he worked on, just the same.

Suddenly he heard a shriek, and he flung the spade from him and started for the bridge, looking up like a startled deer. Ah, there was Winifred – Joyce had hurt herself. He went on up the garden.

'What is it?'

The child was still screaming – now it was 'Daddy! Daddy! Oh – oh, Daddy!' And the mother was saying, 'Don't be frightened, darling. Let mother look.'

But the child only cried, 'Oh, Daddy, Daddy, Daddy!'

She was terrified by the sight of the blood running from her own knee. Winifred crouched down, with her child of six in her lap, to examine the knee. Egbert bent over also.

'Don't make such a noise, Joyce,' he said irritably. 'How did she do it?'

'She fell on that sickle thing which you left lying about after cutting the grass,' said Winifred, looking into his face with bitter accusation as he bent near.

He had taken his handkerchief and tied it round the knee. Then he lifted the still sobbing child in his arms, and carried her into the house and upstairs to her bed. In his arms she became quiet. But his heart was burning with pain and with guilt. He had left the sickle there lying on the edge of the grass, and so his first-born child whom he loved so dearly had come to hurt. But then it was an accident – it was an accident. Why should he feel guilty? It would probably be nothing, better in two or three days. Why take it to heart, why worry? He put it aside.

The child lay on the bed in her little summer frock, her face very white now after the shock. Nurse had come carrying the youngest child: and little Annabel stood holding her skirt. Winifred, terribly serious and wooden-seeming, was bending over the knee, from which she had taken his blood-soaked handkerchief. Egbert bent forward, too, keeping more sangfroid in his face than in his heart. Winifred went all of a lump of seriousness, so he had to keep some reserve. The child moaned and whimpered.

The knee was still bleeding profusely – it was a deep cut right in the joint.

'You'd better go for the doctor, Egbert,' said Winifred bitterly.

'Oh, no! Oh, no!' cried Joyce in a panic.

'Joyce, my darling, don't cry!' said Winifred, suddenly catching the little girl to her breast in a strange tragic anguish, the Mater Dolorata[3]. Even the child was frightened into silence. Egbert looked at the tragic figure of his wife with the child at her breast, and turned away. Only Annabel started suddenly to cry: 'Joycey, Joycey, don't have your leg bleeding!'

Egbert rode four miles to the village for the doctor. He could not help feeling that Winifred was laying it on rather. Surely the knee itself wasn't hurt! Surely not. It was only a surface cut.

The doctor was out. Egbert left the message and came cycling swiftly home, his heart pinched with anxiety. He dropped sweating off his bicycle and went into the house, looking rather small, like a man who is at fault. Winifred was upstairs sitting by Joyce, who was looking pale and important in bed, and was eating some tapioca pudding. The pale, small, scared face of his child went to Egbert's heart.

'Doctor Wing was out. He'll be here about half-past two,' said Egbert.

'I don't want him to come,' whimpered Joyce.

'Joyce, dear, you must be patient and quiet,' said Winifred. 'He won't hurt you. But he will tell us what to do to make your knee better quickly. That is why he must come.'

Winifred always explained carefully to her little girls, and it always took the words off their lips for the moment.

'Does it bleed yet?' said Egbert.

Winifred moved the bedclothes carefully aside.

'I think not,' she said.

Egbert stooped also to look.

'No, it doesn't,' she said. Then he stood up with a relieved look on his face. He turned to the child.

'Eat your pudding, Joyce,' he said. 'It won't be anything. You've only got to keep still for a few days.'

'You haven't had your dinner, have you, Daddy?'

'Not yet.'

'Nurse will give it to you,' said Winifred.

'You'll be all right, Joyce,' he said, smiling to the child and pushing the blonde hair off her brow. She smiled back winsomely into his face.

He went downstairs and ate his meal alone. Nurse served him. She liked waiting on him. All women liked him and liked to do things for him.

The doctor came – a fat country practitioner, pleasant and kind.

'What, little girl, been tumbling down, have you? There's a thing to be doing, for a smart little lady like you! What! And cutting your knee! Tut-tut-tut! That *wasn't* clever of you, now was it? Never mind, never mind, soon be better. Let us look at it. Won't hurt you. Not the least in life. Bring a bowl with a little warm water, nurse. Soon have it all right again, soon have it all right.'

Joyce smiled at him with a pale smile of faint superiority. This was *not* the way in which she was used to being talked to.

He bent down, carefully looking at the little, thin, wounded knee of the child. Egbert bent over him.

'Oh, dear, oh, dear! Quite a deep little cut. Nasty little cut. Nasty little cut. But, never mind. Never mind, little lady. We'll soon have it better. Soon have it better, little lady. What's your name?'

'My name is Joyce,' said the child distinctly.

'Oh, really!' he replied. 'Oh, really! Well, that's a fine name too, in my opinion. Joyce, eh? – And how old might Miss Joyce be? Can she tell me that?'

'I'm six,' said the child, slightly amused and very condescending.

'Six! There now. Add up and count as far as six, can you? Well, that's a clever little girl, a clever little girl. And if she has to drink a spoonful of medicine, she won't make a murmur, I'll be bound. Not like *some* little girls. What? Eh?'

'I take it if mother wishes me to,' said Joyce.

'Ah, there now! That's the style! That's what I like to hear from a little lady in bed because she's cut her knee. That's the style –'

The comfortable and prolix doctor dressed and bandaged the knee and recommended bed and a light diet for the little lady. He thought a week or a fortnight would put it right. No bones or ligatures damaged – fortunately. Only a flesh cut. He would come again in a day or two.

So Joyce was reassured and stayed in bed and had all her toys up. Her father often played with her. The doctor came the third day. He was fairly pleased with the knee. It was healing. It was healing – yes – yes. Let the child continue in bed. He came again after a day or two. Winifred was a trifle uneasy. The wound seemed to be healing on the top, but it hurt the child too much. It didn't look quite right. She said so to Egbert.

'Egbert, I'm sure Joyce's knee isn't healing properly.'

'I think it is,' he said. 'I think it's all right.'

'I'd rather Doctor Wing came again – I don't feel satisfied.'

'Aren't you trying to imagine it worse than it really is?'

'You would say so, of course. But I shall write a postcard to Doctor Wing now.'

The doctor came next day. He examined the knee. Yes, there was inflammation. Yes, there *might* be a little septic poisoning – there might. There might. Was the child feverish?

So a fortnight passed by, and the child *was* feverish, and the knee was more inflamed and grew worse and was painful, painful. She cried in the night, and her mother had to sit up with her. Egbert still insisted it was nothing, really – it would pass. But in his heart he was anxious.

Winifred wrote again to her father. On Saturday the elderly man appeared. And no sooner did Winifred see the thick, rather short figure in its grey suit than a great yearning came over her.

'Father, I'm not satisfied with Joyce. I'm not satisfied with Doctor Wing.'

'Well, Winnie, dear, if you're not satisfied we must have further advice, that is all.'

The sturdy, powerful, elderly man went upstairs, his voice sounding rather grating through the house, as if it cut upon the tense atmosphere.

'How are you, Joyce, darling?' he said to the child. 'Does your knee hurt you? Does it hurt you, dear?'

'It does sometimes.' The child was shy of him, cold towards him.

'Well, dear, I'm sorry for that. I hope you try to bear it, and not trouble mother too much.'

There was no answer. He looked at the knee. It was red and stiff.

'Of course,' he said, 'I think we must have another doctor's opinion. And if we're going to have it, we had better have it at once. Egbert, do you think you might cycle in to Bingham for Doctor Wayne? I found him very satisfactory for Winnie's mother.'

'I can go if you think it necessary,' said Egbert.

'Certainly I think it necessary. Even if there is nothing, we can have peace of mind. Certainly I think it necessary. I should like Doctor Wayne to come this evening if possible.'

So Egbert set off on his bicycle through the wind, like a boy sent on an errand, leaving his father-in-law a pillar of assurance, with Winifred.

Doctor Wayne came, and looked grave. Yes, the knee was certainly taking the wrong way. The child might be lame for life.

Up went the fire and fear and anger in every heart. Doctor Wayne came again the next day for a proper examination. And, yes, the knee had really taken bad ways. It should be X-rayed. It was very important.

Godfrey Marshall walked up and down the lane with the doctor, beside the standing motor car: up and down, up and down in one of those consultations of which he had had so many in his life.

As a result he came indoors to Winifred.

'Well, Winnie, dear, the best thing to do is to take Joyce up to London, to a nursing home where she can have proper treatment. Of course this knee has been allowed to go wrong. And apparently there is a risk that the child may even lose her leg. What do you think, dear? You agree to our taking her up to town and putting her under the best care?'

'Oh, Father, you *know* I would do anything on earth for her.'

'I know you would, Winnie darling. The pity is that there has been this unfortunate delay already. I can't think what Doctor Wing was doing. Apparently the child is in danger of losing her leg. Well then, if you will have everything ready, we will take her up to town tomorrow. I will order the large car from Denley's to be here at ten. Egbert, will you take a telegram at once to Doctor Jackson? It is a small nursing home for children and for surgical cases, not far from Baker Street. I'm sure Joyce will be all right there.'

'Oh, Father, can't I nurse her myself!'

'Well, darling, if she is to have proper treatment, she had best be in a home. The X-ray treatment, and the electric treatment, and whatever is necessary.'

'It will cost a great deal –' said Winifred.

'We can't think of cost, if the child's leg is in danger – or even her life. No use speaking of cost,' said the elder man impatiently.

And so it was. Poor Joyce, stretched out on a bed in the big closed motor car – the mother sitting by her head, the grand-father in his short grey beard and a bowler hat, sitting by her feet, thick, and implacable in his responsibility – they rolled slowly away from Crockham, and from Egbert who stood there bareheaded and a little ignominious, left behind. He was to shut up the house and bring the rest of the family back to town, by train, the next day.

Followed a dark and bitter time. The poor child. The poor, poor child, how she suffered, an agony and a long crucifixion in that nursing home. It was a bitter six weeks which changed the soul of Winifred for ever. As she sat by the bed of her poor, tortured little child, tortured with the agony of the knee, and the still worse agony of these diabolic, but perhaps necessary modern treatments, she felt her heart killed and going cold in her breast. Her little Joyce, her frail, brave, wonderful, little Joyce, frail and small and pale as a white flower! Ah, how had she, Winifred, dared to be so wicked, so wicked, so careless, so sensual.

'Let my heart die! Let my woman's heart of flesh die! Saviour, let my heart die. And save my child. Let my heart die from the world and from the flesh. Oh, destroy my heart that is so wayward. Let my heart of pride die. Let my heart die.'

So she prayed beside the bed of her child. And like the Mother with the seven swords in her breast,[4] slowly her heart of pride and passion died in her breast, bleeding away. Slowly it died, bleeding away, and she turned to the Church for comfort, to Jesus, to the Mother of God, but most of all, to that great and enduring institution, the Roman Catholic Church. She withdrew into the shadow of the Church. She was a mother with three children. But in her soul she died, her heart of pride and passion and desire bled to death, her soul belonged to her Church, her body belonged to her duty as a mother.

Her duty as a wife did not enter. As a wife she had no sense of duty, only a certain bitterness towards the man with whom she had known such sensuality and distraction. She was purely the Mater Dolorata. To the man she was closed as a tomb.

Egbert came to see his child. But Winifred seemed to be always seated there, like the tomb of his manhood and his fatherhood. Poor Winifred: she was still young, still strong and ruddy and beautiful like a ruddy hard flower of the field. Strange – her ruddy, healthy face, so sombre, and her strong, heavy, full-blooded body, so still. She, a nun! Never. And yet the gates of her heart and soul had shut in his face with a slow, resonant clang, shutting him out for ever. There was no need for her to go into a convent. Her will had done it.

And between this young mother and this young father lay the crippled child, like a bit of pale silk floss on the pillow, and a little white pain-quenched face. He could not bear it. He just could not bear it. He turned aside. There was nothing to do but to turn aside. He turned aside, and went hither and thither, desultory. He was still attractive and desirable. But there was a little frown between his brow as if he had been cleft there with a hatchet – cleft right in, for ever, and that was the stigma.

The child's leg was saved, but the knee was locked stiff. The fear now was lest the lower leg should wither, or cease to grow. There must be long-continued massage and treatment, daily treatment, even when the child left the nursing home. And the whole of the expense was borne by the grandfather.

Egbert now had no real home. Winifred with the children and nurse was tied to the little flat in London. He could not live there: he could not contain himself. The cottage was shut up – or lent to friends. He went down sometimes to work in his garden and keep the place in order. Then with the empty house around him at night, all the empty rooms, he felt his heart go wicked. The sense of frustration and futility, like some slow, torpid snake, slowly bit right through his heart. Futility, futility; the horrible marsh-poison went through his veins and killed him.

As he worked in the garden in the silence of day he would listen for a sound. No sound. No sound of Winifred from the dark inside of the cottage; no sound of children's voices from the air, from the common, from the near distance. No sound, nothing but the old dark marsh-venomous atmosphere of the place. So he worked spasmodically through the day, and at night made a fire and cooked some food alone.

He was alone. He himself cleaned the cottage and made his bed. But his mending he did not do. His shirts were slit on the shoulders, when he had been working, and the white flesh showed through. He would feel the air and the spots of rain on his exposed flesh. And he would look again across the common, where the dark, tufted gorse was dying to seed, and the bits of cat-heather were coming pink in tufts, like a sprinkling of sacrificial blood.

His heart went back to the savage old spirit of the place – the desire for old gods, old, lost passions, the passion of the cold-blooded, darting snakes that hissed and shot away from him, the mystery of blood-sacrifices, all the lost, intense sensations of the primeval people of the place, whose passions seethed in the air still, from those long days before the Romans came. The seethe of a lost, dark passion in the air. The presence of unseen snakes.

A queer, baffled, half-wicked look came on his face. He could not stay long at the cottage. Suddenly he must swing on to his bicycle and go – anywhere. Anywhere, away from the place. He would stay a few days with his mother in the old home. His mother adored him and grieved as a mother would. But the little, baffled, half-wicked smile curled on his face, and he swung away from his mother's solicitude as from everything else.

Always moving on – from place to place, friend to friend, and always swinging away from sympathy. As soon as sympathy, like a soft hand, was reached out to touch him, away he swerved, instinctively, as a harmless snake swerves and swerves and swerves away from an outstretched hand. Away he must go. And periodically he went back to Winifred.

He was terrible to her now, like a temptation. She had devoted herself to her children and her Church. Joyce was once more on her feet, but – alas! – lame, with iron supports to her leg and a little crutch. It was strange how she had grown into a long, pallid, wild little thing. Strange that the pain had not made her soft and docile, but had brought out a wild, almost maenad temper in the child. She was seven, and long and white and thin, but by no means subdued. Her blonde hair was darkening. She still had long sufferings to face, and, in her own childish consciousness, the stigma of her lameness to bear.

And she bore it. An almost maenad courage seemed to possess her, as if she were a long, thin, young weapon of life. She acknowledged all her mother's care. She would stand by her mother for ever. But some of her father's fine-tempered desperation flashed in her.

When Egbert saw his little girl limping horribly – not only limping but lurching horribly in crippled, childish way, his heart again hardened with chagrin, like steel that is tempered again. There was a tacit understanding between him and his little girl: not what we would call love, but a weapon-like kinship. There was a tiny touch of irony in his manner towards her, contrasting sharply with Winifred's heavy, unleavened solicitude and care. The child flickered back to him with an answering little smile of irony and recklessness, an odd flippancy which made Winifred only the more sombre and earnest.

The Marshalls took endless thought and trouble for the child, searching out every means to save her limb and her active freedom. They spared no effort and no money, they spared no strength of will. With all their slow, heavy power of will they willed that Joyce should save her liberty of movement, should win back her wild, free grace. Even if it took a long time to recover, it should be recovered.

So the situation stood. And Joyce submitted, week after week, month after month to the tyranny and pain of the treatment. She acknowledged the honourable effort on her behalf. But her flamy reckless spirit was her father's. It was he who had all the glamour for her. He and she were like members of some forbidden secret society who know one another but may not recognise one another. Knowledge they had in common, the same secret of life, the father and the child. But the child stayed in the camp of her mother, honourably, and the father wandered outside like Ishmael[5], only coming sometimes to sit in the home for an hour or two, an evening or two beside the camp-fire, like Ishmael, in a curious silence and tension, with the mocking answer of the desert speaking out of his silence, and annulling the whole convention of the domestic home.

His presence was almost an anguish to Winifred. She prayed against it. That little cleft between his brow, that flickering, wicked, little smile that seemed to haunt his face, and above all, the triumphant loneliness, the Ishmael quality. And then the erectness of his supple body, like a symbol. The very way he stood, so quiet, so insidious, like an erect, supple symbol of life, the living body, confronting her downcast soul, was torture to her. He was like a supple living idol moving before her eyes, and she felt if she watched him she was damned.

And he came and made himself at home in her little home. When he was there, moving in his own quiet way, she felt as if the whole great law of sacrifice, by which she had elected to live, were annulled. He annulled by his very presence the laws of her life. And what did he substitute? Ah, against that question she hardened herself in recoil.

It was awful to her to have to have him about – moving about in his shirtsleeves, speaking in his tenor, throaty voice to the children. Annabel simply adored him, and he teased the little girl. The baby, Barbara, was not sure of him. She had been born a stranger to him. But even the nurse, when she saw his white shoulder of flesh through the slits of his torn shirt, thought it a shame.

Winifred felt it was only another weapon of his against her.

'You have other shirts – why do you wear that old one that is all torn, Egbert?' she said.

'I may as well wear it out,' he said subtly.

He knew she would not offer to mend it for him. She *could* not. And no, she would not. Had she not her own gods to honour? And could she betray them, submitting to his Baal and Ashtoreth?[6] And it was terrible to her, his unsheathed presence, that seemed to annul her and her faith, like another revelation. Like a gleaming idol evoked against her, a vivid life-idol that might triumph.

He came and he went – and she persisted. And then the Great War broke out. He was a man who could not go to the dogs. He could not dissipate himself. He was pure-bred in his Englishness, and even when he would have killed to be vicious, he could not.

So when the war broke out his whole instinct was against it – against war. He had not the faintest desire to overcome any foreigners or to help in their death. He had no conception of Imperial England, and Rule Britannia was just a joke to him. He was a pure-blooded Englishman, perfect in his race, and when he was truly himself he could no more have been aggressive on the score of his Englishness than a rose can be aggressive on the score of its rosiness.

No, he had no desire to defy Germany and to exalt England. The distinction between German and English was not for him the distinction between good and bad. It was the distinction between blue water flowers and red or white bush blossoms: just difference. The difference between the wild boar and the wild bear. And a man was good or bad according to his nature, not according to his nationality.

Egbert was well bred, and this was part of his natural understanding. It was merely unnatural to him to hate a nation en bloc. Certain individuals he disliked, and others he liked, and the mass he knew nothing about. Certain deeds he disliked, certain deeds seemed natural to him, and about most deeds he had no particular feeling.

He had, however, the one deepest pure-bred instinct. He recoiled inevitably from having his feelings dictated to him by the mass feeling. His feelings were his own, his understanding was his own, and he would never go back on either, willingly. Shall a man become inferior to his own true knowledge and self, just because the mob expects it of him?

What Egbert felt subtly and without question, his father-in-law felt also in a rough, more combative way. Different as the two men were, they were two real Englishmen, and their instincts were almost the same.

And Godfrey Marshall had the world to reckon with. There was German military aggression, and the English non-military idea of liberty and the 'conquests of peace' – meaning industrialism. Even if the choice between militarism and industrialism were a choice of evils, the elderly man asserted his choice of the latter, perforce. He whose soul was quick with the instinct of power.

Egbert just refused to reckon with the world. He just refused even to decide between German militarism and British industrialism. He chose neither. As for atrocities, he despised the people who committed them as inferior criminal types. There was nothing national about crime.

And yet, war! War! Just war! Not right or wrong, but just war itself. Should he join? Should he give himself over to war? The question was in his mind for some weeks. Not because he thought England was right and Germany wrong. Probably Germany was wrong, but he refused to make a choice. Not because he felt inspired. No. But just – war.

The deterrent was the giving himself over into the power of other men, and into the power of the mob spirit of a democratic army. Should he give himself over? Should he make over his own life and body to the control of something which he *knew* was inferior, in spirit, to his own self? Should he commit himself into the power of an inferior control? Should he? Should he betray himself?

He was going to put himself into the power of his inferiors, and he knew it. He was going to subjugate himself. He was going to be ordered about by petty *canaille* of non-commissioned officers – and even commissioned officers. He who was born and bred free. Should he do it?

He went to his wife, to speak to her.

'Shall I join up, Winifred?'

She was silent. Her instinct also was dead against it. And yet a certain profound resentment made her answer:

'You have three children dependent on you. I don't know whether you have thought of that.'

It was still only the third month of the war, and the old pre-war ideas were still alive.

'Of course. But it won't make much difference to them. I shall be earning a shilling a day, at least.'

'You'd better speak to Father, I think,' she replied heavily.

Egbert went to his father-in-law. The elderly man's heart was full of resentment.

'I should say,' he said rather sourly, 'it is the best thing you could do.'

Egbert went and joined up immediately, as a private soldier. He was drafted into the light artillery.

Winifred now had a new duty towards him: the duty of a wife towards a husband who is himself performing his duty towards the world. She loved him still. She would always love him, as far as earthly love went. But it was duty she now lived by. When he came back to her in khaki, a soldier, she submitted to him as a wife. It was her duty. But to his passion she could never again fully submit. Something prevented her, for ever: even her own deepest choice.

He went back again to camp. It did not suit him to be a modern soldier. In the thick, gritty, hideous khaki his subtle physique was extinguished as if he had been killed. In the ugly intimacy of the camp his thoroughbred sensibilities were just degraded. But he had chosen, so he accepted. An ugly little look came onto his face, of a man who has accepted his own degradation.

In the early spring Winifred went down to Crockham to be there when primroses were out, and the tassels hanging on the hazel bushes. She felt something like a reconciliation towards Egbert, now he was a prisoner in camp most of his days. Joyce was wild with delight at seeing the garden and the common again, after the eight or nine months of London and misery. She was still lame. She still had the irons up her leg. But she lurched about with a wild, crippled agility.

Egbert came for a weekend, in his gritty, thick, sandpaper khaki and puttees and the hideous cap. Nay, he looked terrible. And on his face a slightly impure look, a little sore on his lip, as if he had eaten too much or drunk too much or let his blood become a little unclean. He was almost uglily healthy, with the camp life. It did not suit him.

Winifred waited for him in a little passion of duty and sacrifice, willing to serve the soldier, if not the man. It only made him feel a little more ugly inside. The weekend was torment to him: the memory of the camp, the knowledge of the life he led there; even the sight of his own legs in that abhorrent khaki. He felt as if the hideous cloth went into his blood and made it gritty and dirty. Then Winifred so ready to serve the *soldier*, when she repudiated the man. And this made the grit worse between his teeth. And the children running around playing and calling in the rather mincing fashion of children who have nurses and governesses and literature in the family. And Joyce so lame! It had all become unreal to him, after the camp. It only set his soul on edge. He left at dawn on the Monday morning, glad to get back to the realness and vulgarity of the camp.

Winifred would never meet him again at the cottage – only in London, where the world was with them. But sometimes he came alone to Crockham, perhaps when friends were staying there. And then he would work awhile in his garden. This summer still it would flame with blue anchusas and big red poppies; the mulleins would sway their soft, downy erections in the air – he loved mulleins – and the honeysuckle would stream out scent like memory, when the owl was whooing. Then he sat by the fire with the friends and with Winifred's sisters, and they sang the folk-songs. He put on thin civilian clothes and his charm and his beauty and the supple dominancy of his body glowed out again. But Winifred was not there.

At the end of the summer he went to Flanders, into action. He seemed already to have gone out of life, beyond the pale of life. He hardly remembered his life any more, being like a man who is going to take a jump from a height, and is only looking to where he must land.

He was twice slightly wounded, in two months. But not enough to put him off duty for more than a day or two. They were retiring again, holding the enemy back. He was in the rear – three machine guns. The country was all pleasant, war had not yet trampled it. Only the air seemed shattered, and the land awaiting death. It was a small, unimportant action in which he was engaged.

The guns were stationed on a little bushy hillock just outside a village. But occasionally it was difficult to say from which direction came the sharp crackle of rifle fire, and beyond, the far-off thud of cannon. The afternoon was wintry and cold.

A lieutenant stood on a little iron platform at the top of the ladders, taking the sights and giving the aim, calling in a high, tense, mechanical voice. Out of the sky came the sharp cry of the directions, then the warning numbers, then 'fire!' The shot went, the piston of the gun sprang back, there was a sharp explosion, and a very faint film of smoke in the air. Then the other two guns fired, and there was a lull. The officer was uncertain of the enemy's position. The thick clump of horse chestnut trees below was without change. Only in the far distance the sound of heavy firing continued, so far off as to give a sense of peace.

The gorse bushes on either hand were dark, but a few sparks of flowers showed yellow. He noticed them almost unconsciously as he waited, in the lull. He was in his shirtsleeves, and the air came chill on his arms. Again his shirt was slit on the shoulders, and the flesh showed through. He was dirty and unkempt. But his face was quiet. So many things go out of consciousness before we come to the end of consciousness.

Before him, below, was the high road, running between high banks of grass and gorse. He saw the whitish muddy tracks and deep scores in the road, where the part of the regiment had retired. Now all was still. Sounds that came, came from the outside. The place where he stood was still silent, chill, serene; the white church among the trees beyond seemed like a thought only.

He moved into a lightning-like mechanical response at the sharp cry from the officer overhead. Mechanism, the pure mechanical action of obedience at the guns. Pure mechanical action at the guns. It left the soul unburdened, brooding in dark nakedness. In the end, the soul is alone, brooding on the face of the uncreated flux, as a bird on a dark sea.

Nothing could be seen but the road, and a crucifix knocked slanting and the dark, autumnal fields and woods. There appeared three horsemen on a little eminence, very small, on the crest of a ploughed field. They were our own men. Of the enemy, nothing.

The lull continued. Then suddenly came sharp orders, and a new direction of the guns, and an intense, exciting activity. Yet at the centre the soul remained dark and aloof, alone.

But even so, it was the soul that heard the new sound – the new, deep 'papp!' of a gun that seemed to touch right upon the soul. He kept up the rapid activity at the machine gun, sweating. But in his soul was the echo of the new, deep sound, deeper than life.

And in confirmation came the awful faint whistling of a shell, advancing almost suddenly into a piercing, tearing shriek that would tear through the membrane of life. He heard it in his ears, but he heard it also in his soul, in tension. There was relief when the thing had swung by and struck, away beyond. He heard the hoarseness of its explosion, and the voice of the soldier calling to the horses. But he did not turn round to look. He only noticed a twig of holly with red berries fall like a gift on to the road below.

Not this time, not this time. Whither thou goest I will go. Did he say it to the shell, or to whom? Whither thou goest I will go. Then, the faint whistling of another shell dawned, and his blood became small and still to receive it. It drew nearer, like some horrible blast of wind; his blood lost consciousness. But in the second of suspension he saw the heavy shell swoop to earth, into the rocky bushes on the right, and earth and stones poured up into the sky. It was as if he heard no sound. The earth and stones and fragments of bush fell to earth again, and there was the same unchanging peace. The Germans had got the aim.

Would they move now? Would they retire? Yes. The officer was giving the last lightning-rapid orders to fire before withdrawing. A shell passed unnoticed in the rapidity of action. And then, into the silence, into the suspense where the soul brooded, finally crashed a noise and a darkness and a moment's flaming agony and horror. Ah, he had seen the dark bird flying towards him, flying home this time. In one instant life and eternity went up in a conflagration of agony, then there was a weight of darkness.

When faintly something began to struggle in the darkness, a consciousness of himself, he was aware of a great load and a clanging sound. To have known the moment of death! And to be forced, before dying, to review it. So, fate, even in death.

There was a resounding of pain. It seemed to sound from the outside of his consciousness, like a loud bell clanging very near. Yet he knew it was himself. He must associate himself with it. After a lapse and a new effort, he identified a pain in his head, a large pain that clanged and resounded. So far he could identify himself with himself. Then there was a lapse.

After a time he seemed to wake up again, and waking, to know that he was at the front, and that he was killed. He did not open his eyes. Light was not yet his. The clanging pain in his head rang out the rest of his consciousness. So he lapsed away from consciousness, in unutterable sick abandon of life.

Bit by bit, like a doom came the necessity to know. He was hit in the head. It was only a vague surmise at first. But in the swinging of the pendulum of pain, swinging ever nearer and nearer, to touch him into an agony of consciousness and a consciousness of agony, gradually the knowledge emerged – he must be hit in the head – hit on the left brow; if so, there would be blood – was there blood? – could he feel blood in his left eye? Then the clanging seemed to burst the membrane of his brain, like death-madness.

Was there blood on his face? Was hot blood flowing? Or was it dry blood congealing down his cheek? It took him hours even to ask the question, time being no more than an agony in darkness, without measurement.

A long time after he had opened his eyes he realised he was seeing something – something, something, but the effort to recall what was too great. No, no; no recall!

Were they the stars in the dark sky? Was it possible it was stars in the dark sky? Stars? The world? Ah, no, he could not know it! Stars and the world were gone for him, he closed his eyes. No stars, no sky, no world. No, no! The thick darkness of blood alone. It should be one great lapse into the thick darkness of blood in agony.

Death, oh, death! The world all blood, and the blood all writhing with death. The soul like the tiniest little light out on a dark sea, the sea of blood. And the light guttering, beating, pulsing in a windless storm, wishing it could go out, yet unable.

There had been life. There had been Winifred and his children. But the frail death-agony effort to catch at straws of memory, straws of life from the past, brought on too great a nausea. No, no! No Winifred, no children. No world, no people. Better the agony of dissolution ahead than the nausea of the effort backwards. Better the terrible work should go forward, the dissolving into the black sea of death, in the extremity of dissolution, than that there should be any reaching back towards life. To forget! To forget! Utterly, utterly to forget, in the great forgetting of death. To break the core and the unit of life, and to lapse out on the great darkness. Only that. To break the clue, and mingle and commingle with the one darkness, without afterwards or forwards. Let the black sea of death itself solve the problem of futurity. Let the will of man break and give up.

What was that? A light! A terrible light! Was it figures? Was it legs of a horse colossal – colossal above him, huge, huge?

The Germans heard a slight noise, and started. Then, in the glare of a light-bomb, by the side of the heap of earth thrown up by the shell, they saw the dead face.

The Blind Man

Isabel Pervin was listening for two sounds – for the sound of wheels on the drive outside and for the noise of her husband's footsteps in the hall. Her dearest and oldest friend, a man who seemed almost indispensable to her living, would drive up in the rainy dusk of the closing November day. The trap had gone to fetch him from the station. And her husband, who had been blinded in Flanders, and who had a disfiguring mark on his brow, would be coming in from the outhouses.

He had been home for a year now. He was totally blind. Yet they had been very happy. The Grange was Maurice's own place. The back was a farmstead, and the Wernhams, who occupied the rear premises, acted as farmers. Isabel lived with her husband in the handsome rooms in front. She and he had been almost entirely alone together since he was wounded. They talked and sang and read together in a wonderful and unspeakable intimacy. Then she reviewed books for a Scottish newspaper, carrying on her old interest, and he occupied himself a good deal with the farm. Sightless, he could still discuss everything with Wernham, and he could also do a good deal of work about the place – menial work, it is true, but it gave him satisfaction. He milked the cows, carried in the pails, turned the separator, attended to the pigs and horses. Life was still very full and strangely serene for the blind man, peaceful with the almost incomprehensible peace of immediate contact in darkness. With his wife he had a whole world, rich and real and invisible.

They were newly and remotely happy. He did not even regret the loss of his sight in these times of dark, palpable joy. A certain exultance swelled his soul.

But as time wore on, sometimes the rich glamour would leave them. Sometimes, after months of this intensity, a sense of burden overcame Isabel, a weariness, a terrible *ennui*, in that silent house approached between a colonnade of tall-shafted pines. Then she felt she would go mad, for she could not bear it.

And sometimes he had devastating fits of depression, which seemed to lay waste his whole being. It was worse than depression – a black misery, when his own life was a torture to him, and when his presence was unbearable to his wife. The dread went down to the roots of her soul as these black days recurred. In a kind of panic she tried to wrap herself up still further in her husband. She forced the old spontaneous cheerfulness and joy to continue. But the effort it cost her was almost too much. She knew she could not keep it up. She felt she would scream with the strain, and would give anything, anything, to escape. She longed to possess her husband utterly; it gave her inordinate joy to have him entirely to herself. And yet, when again he was gone in a black and massive misery, she could not bear him, she could not bear herself; she wished she could be snatched away off the earth altogether, anything rather than live at this cost.

Dazed, she schemed for a way out. She invited friends, she tried to give him some further connection with the outer world. But it was no good. After all their joy and suffering, after their dark, great year of blindness and solitude and unspeakable nearness, other people seemed to them both shallow, prattling, rather impertinent. Shallow prattle seemed presumptuous. He became impatient and irritated, she was wearied. And so they lapsed into their solitude again. For they preferred it.

But now, in a few weeks' time, her second baby would be born. The first had died, an infant, when her husband first went out to France. She looked with joy and relief to the coming of the second. It would be her salvation. But also she felt some anxiety. She was thirty years old, her husband was a year younger. They both wanted the child very much. Yet she could not help feeling afraid. She had her husband on her hands, a terrible joy to her, and a terrifying burden. The child would occupy her love and attention. And then, what of Maurice? What would he do? If only she could feel that he, too, would be at peace and happy when the child came! She did so want to luxuriate in a rich, physical satisfaction of maternity. But the man, what would he do? How could she provide for him, how avert those shattering black moods of his, which destroyed them both?

She sighed with fear. But at this time Bertie Reid wrote to Isabel. He was her old friend, a second or third cousin, a Scotchman, as she was a Scotchwoman. They had been brought up near to one another, and all her life he had been her friend, like a brother, but better than her own brothers. She loved him – though not in the marrying sense. There was a sort of kinship between them, an affinity. They understood one another instinctively. But Isabel would never have thought of marrying Bertie. It would have seemed like marrying in her own family.

Bertie was a barrister and a man of letters, a Scotchman of the intellectual type, quick, ironical, sentimental, and on his knees before the woman he adored but did not want to marry. Maurice Pervin was different. He came of a good old country family – the Grange was not a very great distance from Oxford. He was passionate, sensitive, perhaps over-sensitive, wincing – a big fellow with heavy limbs and a forehead that flushed painfully. For his mind was slow, as if drugged by the strong provincial blood that beat in his veins. He was very sensitive to his own mental slowness, his feelings being quick and acute. So that he was just the opposite to Bertie, whose mind was much quicker than his emotions, which were not so very fine.

From the first the two men did not like each other. Isabel felt that they *ought* to get on together. But they did not. She felt that if only each could have the clue to the other there would be such a rare understanding between them. It did not come off, however. Bertie adopted a slightly ironical attitude, very offensive to Maurice, who returned the Scotch irony with English resentment, a resentment which deepened sometimes into stupid hatred.

This was a little puzzling to Isabel. However, she accepted it in the course of things. Men were made freakish and unreasonable. Therefore, when Maurice was going out to France for the second time, she felt that, for her husband's sake, she must discontinue her friendship with Bertie. She wrote to the barrister to this effect. Bertram Reid simply replied that in this, as in all other matters, he must obey her wishes, if these were indeed her wishes.

For nearly two years nothing had passed between the two friends. Isabel rather gloried in the fact; she had no compunction. She had one great article of faith, which was, that husband and wife should be so important to one another, that the rest of the world simply did not count. She and Maurice were husband and wife. They loved one another. They would have children. Then let everybody and everything else fade into insignificance outside this connubial felicity. She professed herself quite happy and ready to receive Maurice's friends. She was happy and ready: the happy wife, the ready woman in possession. Without knowing why, the friends retired abashed and came no more. Maurice, of course, took as much satisfaction in this connubial absorption as Isabel did.

He shared in Isabel's literary activities, she cultivated a real interest in agriculture and cattle-raising. For she, being at heart perhaps an emotional enthusiast, always cultivated the practical side of life, and prided herself on her mastery of practical affairs. Thus the husband and wife had spent the five years of their married life. The last had been one of blindness and unspeakable intimacy. And now Isabel felt a great indifference coming over her, a sort of lethargy. She wanted to be allowed to bear her child in peace, to nod by the fire and drift vaguely, physically, from day to day. Maurice was like an ominous thundercloud. She had to keep waking up to remember him.

When a little note came from Bertie, asking if he were to put up a tombstone to their dead friendship, and speaking of the real pain he felt on account of her husband's loss of sight, she felt a pang, a fluttering agitation of re-awakening. And she read the letter to Maurice.

'Ask him to come down,' he said.

'Ask Bertie to come here!' she re-echoed.

'Yes – if he wants to.'

Isabel paused for a few moments.

'I know he wants to – he'd only be too glad,' she replied. 'But what about you, Maurice? How would you like it?'

'I should like it.'

'Well – in that case – But I thought you didn't care for him –'

'Oh, I don't know. I might think differently of him now,' the blind man replied. It was rather abstruse to Isabel.

'Well, dear,' she said, 'if you're quite sure –'

'I'm sure enough. Let him come,' said Maurice.

So Bertie was coming, coming this evening, in the November rain and darkness. Isabel was agitated, racked with her old restlessness and indecision. She had always suffered from this pain of doubt, just an agonising sense of uncertainty. It had begun to pass off, in the lethargy of maternity. Now it returned, and she resented it. She struggled as usual to maintain her calm, composed, friendly bearing, a sort of mask she wore over all her body.

A woman had lighted a tall lamp beside the table, and spread the cloth. The long dining room was dim, with its elegant but rather severe pieces of old furniture. Only the round table glowed softly under the light. It had a rich, beautiful effect. The white cloth glistened and dropped its heavy, pointed lace corners almost to the carpet, the china was old and handsome, creamy yellow, with a blotched pattern of harsh red and deep blue, the cups large and bell-shaped, the teapot gallant. Isabel looked at it with superficial appreciation.

Her nerves were hurting her. She looked automatically again at the high, uncurtained windows. In the last dusk she could just perceive outside a huge fir tree swaying its boughs; it was as if she thought it rather than saw it. The rain came flying on the window-panes. Ah, why had she no peace? These two men, why did they tear at her? Why did they not come – why was there this suspense?

She sat in a lassitude that was really suspense and irritation. Maurice, at least, might come in – there was nothing to keep him out. She rose to her feet. Catching sight of her reflection in a mirror, she glanced at herself with a slight smile of recognition, as if she were an old friend to herself. Her face was oval and calm, her nose a little arched. Her neck made a beautiful line down to her shoulder. With hair knotted loosely behind, she had something of a warm, maternal look. Thinking this of herself, she arched her eyebrows and her rather heavy eyelids, with a little flicker of a smile, and for a moment her grey eyes looked amused and wicked, a little sardonic, out of her transfigured Madonna face.

Then, resuming her air of womanly patience – she was really fatally self-determined – she went with a little jerk towards the door. Her eyes were slightly reddened.

She passed down the wide hall, and through a door at the end. Then she was in the farm premises. The scent of dairy, and of farm kitchen, and of farmyard and of leather almost overcame her, but particularly the scent of dairy. They had been scalding out the pans. The flagged passage in front of her was dark, puddled and wet. Light came out from the open kitchen door. She went forward and stood in the doorway. The farm people were at tea, seated at a little distance from her, round a long, narrow table, in the centre of which stood a white lamp. Ruddy faces, ruddy hands holding food, red mouths working, heads bent over the teacups: men, land-girls, boys; it was teatime, feeding-time. Some faces caught sight of her. Mrs Wernham, going round behind the chairs with a large black teapot, halting slightly in her walk, was not aware of her for a moment. Then she turned suddenly.

'Oh, is it madam!' she exclaimed. 'Come in, then, come in! We're at tea.' And she dragged forward a chair.

'No, I won't come in,' said Isabel, 'I'm afraid I interrupt your meal.'

'No – no – not likely, madam, not likely.'

'Hasn't Mr Pervin come in, do you know?'

'I'm sure I couldn't say! Missed him, have you, madam?'

'No, I only wanted him to come in,' laughed Isabel, as if shyly.

'Wanted him, did ye? Get you, boy – get up, now –'

Mrs Wernham knocked one of the boys on the shoulder. He began to scrape to his feet, chewing largely.

'I believe he's in top stable,' said another face from the table.

'Ah! No, don't get up. I'm going myself,' said Isabel.

'Don't you go out of a dirty night like this. Let the lad go. Get along wi' ye, boy,' said Mrs Wernham.

'No, no,' said Isabel, with a decision that was always obeyed. 'Go on with your tea, Tom. I'd like to go across to the stable, Mrs Wernham.'

'Did ever you hear tell!' exclaimed the woman.

'Isn't the trap late?' asked Isabel.

'Why, no,' said Mrs Wernham, peering into the distance at the tall, dim clock. 'No, madam – we can give it another quarter or twenty minutes yet, good – yes, every bit of a quarter.'

'Ah! It seems late when darkness falls so early,' said Isabel.

'It do, that it do. Bother the days, that they draw in so,' answered Mrs Wernham. 'Proper miserable!'

'They are,' said Isabel, withdrawing.

She pulled on her overshoes, wrapped a large tartan shawl around her, put on a man's felt hat, and ventured out along the causeways of the first yard. It was very dark. The wind was roaring in the great elms behind the outhouses. When she came to the second yard the darkness seemed deeper. She was unsure of her footing. She wished she had brought a lantern. Rain blew against her. Half she liked it, half she felt unwilling to battle.

She reached at last the just-visible door of the stable. There was no sign of a light anywhere. Opening the upper half, she looked in – into a simple well of darkness. The smell of horses, and ammonia, and of warmth was startling to her in that full night. She listened with all her ears, but could hear nothing save the night, and the stirring of a horse.

'Maurice!' she called, softly and musically, though she was afraid. 'Maurice – are you there?'

Nothing came from the darkness. She knew the rain and wind blew in upon the horses, the hot animal life. Feeling it wrong, she entered the stable, and drew the lower half of the door shut, holding the upper part close. She did not stir, because she was aware of the presence of the dark hindquarters of the horses, though she could not see them, and she was afraid. Something wild stirred in her heart.

She listened intensely. Then she heard a small noise in the distance – far away, it seemed – the chink of a pan, and a man's voice speaking a brief word. It would be Maurice, in the other part of the stable. She stood motionless, waiting for him to come through the partition door. The horses were so terrifyingly near to her, in the invisible.

The loud jarring of the inner door latch made her start; the door was opened. She could hear and feel her husband entering and invisibly passing among the horses near to her, in darkness as they were, actively intermingled. The rather low sound of his voice as he spoke to the horses came velvety to her nerves. How near he was, and how invisible! The darkness seemed to be in a strange swirl of violent life, just upon her. She turned giddy.

Her presence of mind made her call, quietly and musically:

'Maurice! Maurice – dea-ar!'

'Yes,' he answered. 'Isabel?'

She saw nothing, and the sound of his voice seemed to touch her.

'Hello!' she answered cheerfully, straining her eyes to see him. He was still busy, attending to the horses near her, but she saw only darkness. It made her almost desperate.

'Won't you come in, dear?' she said.

'Yes, I'm coming. Just half a minute. *Stand over – now!* Trap's not come, has it?'

'Not yet,' said Isabel.

His voice was pleasant and ordinary, but it had a slight suggestion of the stable to her. She wished he would come away. Whilst he was so utterly invisible she was afraid of him.

'How's the time?' he asked.

'Not yet six,' she replied. She disliked to answer into the dark. Presently he came very near to her, and she retreated out of doors.

'The weather blows in here,' he said, coming steadily forward, feeling for the doors. She shrank away. At last she could dimly see him.

'Bertie won't have much of a drive,' he said, as he closed the doors.

'He won't indeed!' said Isabel calmly, watching the dark shape at the door.

'Give me your arm, dear,' she said.

She pressed his arm close to her, as she went. But she longed to see him, to look at him. She was nervous. He walked erect, with face rather lifted, but with a curious tentative movement of his powerful, muscular legs. She could feel the clever, careful, strong contact of his feet with the earth, as she balanced against him. For a moment he was a tower of darkness to her, as if he rose out of the earth.

In the house passage he wavered and went cautiously, with a curious look of silence about him as he felt for the bench. Then he sat down heavily. He was a man with rather sloping shoulders, but with heavy limbs, powerful legs that seemed to know the earth. His head was small, usually carried high and light. As he bent down to unfasten his gaiters and boots he did not look blind. His hair was brown and crisp, his hands were large, reddish, intelligent, the veins stood out in the wrists, and his thighs and knees seemed massive. When he stood up his face and neck were surcharged with blood, the veins stood out on his temples. She did not look at his blindness.

Isabel was always glad when they had passed through the dividing door into their own regions of repose and beauty. She was a little afraid of him, out there in the animal grossness of the back. His bearing also changed, as he smelt the familiar, indefinable odour that pervaded his wife's surroundings, a delicate, refined scent, very faintly spicy. Perhaps it came from the pot-pourri bowls.

He stood at the foot of the stairs, arrested, listening. She watched him, and her heart sickened. He seemed to be listening to fate.

'He's not here yet,' he said. 'I'll go up and change.'

'Maurice,' she said, 'you're not wishing he wouldn't come, are you?'

'I couldn't quite say,' he answered. 'I feel myself rather on the qui vive.'

'I can see you are,' she answered. And she reached up and kissed his cheek. She saw his mouth relax into a slow smile.

'What are you laughing at?' she said roguishly.

'You consoling me,' he answered.

'Nay,' she answered. 'Why should I console you? You know we love each other – you know *how* married we are! What does anything else matter?'

'Nothing at all, my dear.'

He felt for her face, and touched it, smiling.

'*You're* all right, aren't you?' he asked, anxiously.

'I'm wonderfully all right, love,' she answered. 'It's you I am a little troubled about, at times.'

'Why me?' he said, touching her cheeks delicately with the tips of his fingers. The touch had an almost hypnotising effect on her.

He went away upstairs. She saw him mount into the darkness, unseeing and unchanging. He did not know that the lamps on the upper corridor were unlighted. He went on into the darkness with unchanging step. She heard him in the bathroom.

Pervin moved about almost unconsciously in his familiar surroundings, dark though everything was. He seemed to know the presence of objects before he touched them. It was a pleasure to him to rock thus through a world of things, carried on the flood in a sort of blood-prescience. He did not think much or trouble much. So long as he kept this sheer immediacy of blood-contact with the substantial world he was happy, he wanted no intervention of visual consciousness. In this state there was a certain rich positivity, bordering sometimes on rapture. Life seemed to move in him like a tide lapping, and advancing, enveloping all things darkly. It was a pleasure to stretch forth the hand and meet the unseen object, clasp it, and possess it in pure contact. He did not try to remember, to visualise. He did not want to. The new way of consciousness substituted itself in him.

The rich suffusion of this state generally kept him happy, reaching its culmination in the consuming passion for his wife. But at times the flow would seem to be checked and thrown back. Then it would beat inside him like a tangled sea, and he was tortured in the shattered chaos of his own blood. He grew to dread this arrest, this throwback, this chaos inside himself, when he seemed merely at the mercy of his own powerful and conflicting elements. How to get some measure of control or surety, this was the question. And when the question rose maddening in him, he would clench his fists as if he would *compel* the whole universe to submit to him. But it was in vain. He could not even compel himself.

Tonight, however, he was still serene, though little tremors of unreasonable exasperation ran through him. He had to handle the razor very carefully, as he shaved, for it was not at one with him, he was afraid of it. His hearing also was too much sharpened. He heard the woman lighting the lamps on the corridor, and attending to the fire in the visitor's room. And then, as he went to his room he heard the trap arrive. Then came Isabel's voice, lifted and calling, like a bell ringing:

'Is it you, Bertie? Have you come?'

And a man's voice answered out of the wind:

'Hello, Isabel. There you are.'

'Have you had a miserable drive? I'm so sorry we couldn't send a closed carriage. I can't see you at all, you know.'

'I'm coming. No, I liked the drive – it was like Perthshire. Well, how are you? You're looking fit as ever, as far as I can see.'

'Oh, yes,' said Isabel. 'I'm wonderfully well. How are you? Rather thin, I think –'

'Worked to death – everybody's old cry. But I'm all right, Ciss. How's Pervin? Isn't he here?'

'Oh, yes, he's upstairs changing. Yes, he's awfully well. Take off your wet things; I'll send them to be dried.'

'And how are you both, in spirits? He doesn't fret?'

'No – no, not at all. No, on the contrary, really. We've been wonderfully happy, incredibly. It's more than I can understand – so wonderful: the nearness, and the peace –'

'Ah! Well, that's awfully good news –'

They moved away. Pervin heard no more. But a childish sense of desolation had come over him, as he heard their brisk voices.

He seemed shut out – like a child that is left out. He was aimless and excluded, he did not know what to do with himself. The helpless desolation came over him. He fumbled nervously as he dressed himself, in a state almost of childishness. He disliked the Scotch accent in Bertie's speech, and the slight response it found on Isabel's tongue. He disliked the slight purr of complacency in the Scottish speech. He disliked intensely the glib way in which Isabel spoke of their happiness and nearness. It made him recoil. He was fretful and beside himself like a child; he had almost a childish nostalgia to be included in the life circle. And at the same time he was a man, dark and powerful and infuriated by his own weakness. By some fatal flaw, he could not be by himself, he had to depend on the support of another. And this very dependence enraged him. He hated Bertie Reid, and at the same time he knew the hatred was nonsense, he knew it was the outcome of his own weakness.

He went downstairs. Isabel was alone in the dining room. She watched him enter, head erect, his feet tentative. He looked so strong-blooded and healthy, and, at the same time, cancelled. Cancelled – that was the word that flew across her mind. Perhaps it was his scars suggested it.

'You heard Bertie come, Maurice?' she said.

'Yes – isn't he here?'

'He's in his room. He looks very thin and worn.'

'I suppose he works himself to death.'

A woman came in with a tray – and after a few minutes Bertie came down. He was a little dark man, with a very big forehead, thin, wispy hair and sad, large eyes. His expression was inordinately sad – almost funny. He had odd, short legs.

Isabel watched him hesitate under the door, and glance nervously at her husband. Pervin heard him and turned.

'Here you are, now,' said Isabel. 'Come, let us eat.'

Bertie went across to Maurice.

'How are you, Pervin,' he said, as he advanced.

The blind man stuck his hand out into space, and Bertie took it.

'Very fit. Glad you've come,' said Maurice.

Isabel glanced at them, and glanced away, as if she could not bear to see them.

'Come,' she said. 'Come to table. Aren't you both awfully hungry? I am, tremendously.'

'I'm afraid you waited for me,' said Bertie, as they sat down.

Maurice had a curious monolithic way of sitting in a chair, erect and distant. Isabel's heart always beat when she caught sight of him thus.

'No,' she replied to Bertie. 'We're very little later than usual. We're having a sort of high tea, not dinner. Do you mind? It gives us such a nice long evening, uninterrupted.'

'I like it,' said Bertie.

Maurice was feeling, with curious little movements, almost like a cat kneading her bed, for his place, his knife and fork, his napkin. He was getting the whole geography of his cover into his consciousness. He sat erect and inscrutable, remote-seeming. Bertie watched the static figure of the blind man, the delicate tactile discernment of the large, ruddy hands, and the curious mindless silence of the brow, above the scar. With difficulty he looked away, and without knowing what he did, picked up a little crystal bowl of violets from the table, and held them to his nose.

'They are sweet-scented,' he said. 'Where do they come from?'

'From the garden – under the windows,' said Isabel.

'So late in the year – and so fragrant! Do you remember the violets under Aunt Bell's south wall?'

The two friends looked at each other and exchanged a smile, Isabel's eyes lighting up.

'Don't I?' she replied. '*Wasn't* she queer!'

'A curious old girl,' laughed Bertie. 'There's a streak of freakishness in the family, Isabel.'

'Ah – but not in you and me, Bertie,' said Isabel. 'Give them to Maurice, will you?' she added, as Bertie was putting down the flowers. 'Have you smelled the violets, dear? Do! – they are so scented.'

Maurice held out his hand, and Bertie placed the tiny bowl against his large, warm-looking fingers. Maurice's hand closed over the thin white fingers of the barrister. Bertie carefully extricated himself. Then the two watched the blind man smelling the violets. He bent his head and seemed to be thinking. Isabel waited.

'Aren't they sweet, Maurice?' she said at last, anxiously.

'Very,' he said. And he held out the bowl. Bertie took it. Both he and Isabel were a little afraid, and deeply disturbed.

The meal continued. Isabel and Bertie chatted spasmodically. The blind man was silent. He touched his food repeatedly, with quick, delicate touches of his knife point, then cut irregular bits. He could not bear to be helped. Both Isabel and Bertie suffered; Isabel wondered why. She did not suffer when she was alone with Maurice. Bertie made her conscious of a strangeness.

After the meal the three drew their chairs to the fire, and sat down to talk. The decanters were put on a table near at hand. Isabel knocked the logs on the fire, and clouds of brilliant sparks went up the chimney. Bertie noticed a slight weariness in her bearing.

'You will be glad when your child comes now, Isabel?' he said.

She looked up to him with a quick wan smile.

'Yes, I shall be glad,' she answered. 'It begins to seem long. Yes, I shall be very glad. So will you, Maurice, won't you?' she added.

'Yes, I shall,' replied her husband.

'We are both looking forward so much to having it,' she said.

'Yes, of course,' said Bertie.

He was a bachelor, three or four years older than Isabel. He lived in beautiful rooms overlooking the river, guarded by a faithful Scottish manservant. And he had his friends among the fair sex – not lovers, friends. So long as he could avoid any danger of courtship or marriage, he adored a few good women with constant and unfailing homage, and he was chivalrously fond of quite a number. But if they seemed to encroach on him, he withdrew and detested them.

Isabel knew him very well, knew his beautiful constancy, and kindness, also his incurable weakness, which made him unable ever to enter into close contact of any sort. He was ashamed of himself, because he could not marry, could not approach women physically. He wanted to do so. But he could not. At the centre of him he was afraid, helplessly and even brutally afraid. He had given up hope, had ceased to expect any more that he could escape his own weakness. Hence he was a brilliant and successful barrister, also littérateur of high repute, a rich man, and a great social success. At the centre he felt himself neuter, nothing.

Isabel knew him well. She despised him even while she admired him. She looked at his sad face, his little short legs, and felt contempt of him. She looked at his dark grey eyes, with their uncanny, almost childlike intuition, and she loved him. He understood amazingly – but she had no fear of his understanding. As a man she patronised him.

And she turned to the impassive, silent figure of her husband. He sat leaning back, with folded arms, and face a little uptilted. His knees were straight and massive. She sighed, picked up the poker, and again began to prod the fire, to rouse the clouds of soft, brilliant sparks.

'Isabel tells me,' Bertie began suddenly, 'that you have not suffered unbearably from the loss of sight.'

Maurice straightened himself to attend, but kept his arms folded.

'No,' he said, 'not unbearably. Now and again one struggles against it, you know. But there are compensations.'

'They say it is much worse to be stone deaf,' said Isabel.

'I believe it is,' said Bertie. 'Are there compensations?' he added, to Maurice.

'Yes. You cease to bother about a great many things.' Again Maurice stretched his figure, stretched the strong muscles of his back, and leaned backwards, with uplifted face.

'And that is a relief,' said Bertie. 'But what is there in place of the bothering? What replaces the activity?'

There was a pause. At length the blind man replied, as out of a negligent, unattentive thinking:

'Oh, I don't know. There's a good deal when you're not active.'

'Is there?' said Bertie. 'What, exactly? It always seems to me that when there is no thought and no action, there is nothing.'

Again Maurice was slow in replying.

'There is something,' he replied. 'I couldn't tell you what it is.'

And the talk lapsed once more, Isabel and Bertie chatting gossip and reminiscence, the blind man silent.

At length Maurice rose restlessly, a big, obtrusive figure. He felt tight and hampered. He wanted to go away.

'Do you mind,' he said, 'if I go and speak to Wernham?'

'No – go along, dear,' said Isabel.

And he went out. A silence came over the two friends. At length Bertie said, 'Nevertheless, it is a great deprivation, Cissie.'

'It is, Bertie. I know it is.'

'Something lacking all the time,' said Bertie.

'Yes, I know. And yet – and yet – Maurice is right. There is something else, something *there*, which you never knew was there, and which you can't express.'

'What is there?' asked Bertie.

'I don't know – it's awfully hard to define it – but something strong and immediate. There's something strange in Maurice's presence – indefinable but I couldn't do without it. I agree that it seems to put one's mind to sleep. But when we're alone I miss nothing; it seems awfully rich, almost splendid, you know.'

'I'm afraid I don't follow,' said Bertie.

They talked desultorily. The wind blew loudly outside, rain chattered on the window-panes, making a sharp, drum sound, because of the closed, mellow-golden shutters inside. The logs burned slowly, with hot, almost invisible small flames. Bertie seemed uneasy, there were dark circles round his eyes. Isabel, rich with her approaching maternity, leaned looking into the fire. Her hair curled in odd, loose strands, very pleasing to the man. But she had a curious feeling of old woe in her heart – old, timeless night-woe.

'I suppose we're all deficient somewhere,' said Bertie.

'I suppose so,' said Isabel wearily.

'Damned, sooner or later.'

'I don't know,' she said, rousing herself. 'I feel quite all right, you know. The child coming seems to make me indifferent to everything, just placid. I can't feel that there's anything to trouble about, you know.'

'A good thing, I should say,' he replied slowly.

'Well, there it is. I suppose it's just nature. If only I felt I needn't trouble about Maurice, I should be perfectly content –'

'But you feel you must trouble about him?'

'Well – I don't know –' She even resented this much effort.

The evening passed slowly. Isabel looked at the clock. 'I say,' she said. 'It's nearly ten o'clock. Where can Maurice be? I'm sure they're all in bed at the back. Excuse me a moment.'

She went out, returning almost immediately.

'It's all shut up and in darkness,' she said. 'I wonder where he is. He must have gone out to the farm –'

Bertie looked at her.

'I suppose he'll come in,' he said.

'I suppose so,' she said. 'But it's unusual for him to be out now.'

'Would you like me to go out and see?'

'Well – if you wouldn't mind. I'd go, but –' She did not want to make the physical effort.

Bertie put on an old overcoat and took a lantern. He went out from the side door. He shrank from the wet and roaring night. Such weather had a nervous effect on him: too much moisture everywhere made him feel almost imbecile. Unwilling, he went through it all. A dog barked violently at him. He peered in all the buildings. At last, as he opened the upper door of a sort of intermediate barn, he heard a grinding noise, and looking in, holding up his lantern, saw Maurice, in his shirtsleeves, standing listening, holding the handle of a turnip pulper. He had been pulping sweet roots, a pile of which lay dimly heaped in a corner behind him.

'That you, Wernham?' said Maurice, listening.

'No, it's me,' said Bertie.

A large, half-wild grey cat was rubbing at Maurice's leg. The blind man stooped to rub its sides. Bertie watched the scene, then unconsciously entered and shut the door behind him, He was in a high sort of barn place, from which, right and left, ran off the corridors in front of the stalled cattle. He watched the slow, stooping motion of the other man, as he caressed the great cat.

Maurice straightened himself.

'You came to look for me?' he said.

'Isabel was a little uneasy,' said Bertie.

'I'll come in. I like messing about doing these jobs.'

The cat had reared her sinister, feline length against his leg, clawing at his thigh affectionately. He lifted her claws out of his flesh.

'I hope I'm not in your way at all at the Grange here,' said Bertie, rather shy and stiff.

'My way? No, not a bit. I'm glad Isabel has somebody to talk to. I'm afraid it's I who am in the way. I know I'm not very lively company. Isabel's all right, don't you think? She's not unhappy, is she?'

'I don't think so.'

'What does she say?'

'She says she's very content – only a little troubled about you.'

'Why me?'

'Perhaps afraid that you might brood,' said Bertie, cautiously.

'She needn't be afraid of that.' He continued to caress the flattened grey head of the cat with his fingers. 'What I am a bit afraid of,' he resumed, 'is that she'll find me a dead weight, always alone with me down here.'

'I don't think you need think that,' said Bertie, though this was what he feared himself.

'I don't know,' said Maurice. 'Sometimes I feel it isn't fair that she's saddled with me.' Then he dropped his voice curiously. 'I say,' he asked, secretly struggling, 'is my face much disfigured? Do you mind telling me?'

'There is the scar,' said Bertie, wondering. 'Yes, it is a disfigurement. But more pitiable than shocking.'

'A pretty bad scar, though,' said Maurice.

'Oh, yes.'

There was a pause.

'Sometimes I feel I am horrible,' said Maurice, in a low voice, talking as if to himself. And Bertie actually felt a quiver of horror.

'That's nonsense,' he said.

Maurice again straightened himself, leaving the cat.

'There's no telling,' he said. Then again, in an odd tone, he added, 'I don't really know you, do I?'

'Probably not,' said Bertie.

'Do you mind if I touch you?'

The lawyer shrank away instinctively. And yet, out of very philanthropy, he said, in a small voice: 'Not at all.'

But he suffered as the blind man stretched out a strong, naked hand to him. Maurice accidentally knocked off Bertie's hat.

'I thought you were taller,' he said, starting. Then he laid his hand on Bertie Reid's head, closing the dome of the skull in a soft, firm grasp, gathering it, as it were; then, shifting his grasp and softly closing again, with a fine, close pressure, till he had covered the skull and the face of the smaller man, tracing the brows, and touching the full, closed eyes, touching the small nose and the nostrils, the rough, short moustache, the mouth, the rather strong chin. The hand of the blind man grasped the shoulder, the arm, the hand of the other man. He seemed to take him, in the soft, travelling grasp.

'You seem young,' he said quietly, at last.

The lawyer stood almost annihilated, unable to answer.

'Your head seems tender, as if you were young,' Maurice repeated. 'So do your hands. Touch my eyes, will you? – touch my scar.'

Now Bertie quivered with revulsion. Yet he was under the power of the blind man, as if hypnotised. He lifted his hand, and laid the fingers on the scar, on the scarred eyes. Maurice suddenly covered them with his own hand, pressed the fingers

83

of the other man upon his disfigured eye sockets, trembling in every fibre, and rocking slightly, slowly, from side to side. He remained thus for a minute or more, whilst Bertie stood as if in a swoon, unconscious, imprisoned.

Then suddenly Maurice removed the hand of the other man from his brow, and stood holding it in his own.

'Oh, my God,' he said, 'we shall know each other now, shan't we? We shall know each other now.'

Bertie could not answer. He gazed mute and terror-struck, overcome by his own weakness. He knew he could not answer. He had an unreasonable fear, lest the other man should suddenly destroy him. Whereas Maurice was actually filled with hot, poignant love, the passion of friendship. Perhaps it was this very passion of friendship which Bertie shrank from most.

'We're all right together now, aren't we?' said Maurice. 'It's all right now, as long as we live, so far as we're concerned?'

'Yes,' said Bertie, trying by any means to escape.

Maurice stood with head lifted, as if listening. The new delicate fulfilment of mortal friendship had come as a revelation and surprise to him, something exquisite and unhoped-for. He seemed to be listening to hear if it were real.

Then he turned for his coat.

'Come,' he said, 'we'll go to Isabel.'

Bertie took the lantern and opened the door. The cat disappeared. The two men went in silence along the causeways. Isabel, as they came, thought their footsteps sounded strange. She looked up pathetically and anxiously for their entrance. There seemed a curious elation about Maurice. Bertie was haggard, with sunken eyes.

'What is it?' she asked.

'We've become friends,' said Maurice, standing with his feet apart, like a strange colossus.

'Friends!' re-echoed Isabel. And she looked again at Bertie. He met her eyes with a furtive, haggard look; his eyes were as if glazed with misery.

'I'm so glad,' she said, in sheer perplexity.

'Yes,' said Maurice.

He was indeed so glad. Isabel took his hand with both hers, and held it fast.

'You'll be happier now, dear,' she said.

But she was watching Bertie. She knew that he had one desire – to escape from this intimacy, this friendship, which had been thrust upon him. He could not bear it that he had been touched by the blind man, his insane reserve broken in. He was like a mollusc whose shell is broken.

You Touched Me

The Pottery House was a square, ugly, brick house girt in by the wall that enclosed the whole grounds of the pottery itself. To be sure, a privet hedge partly masked the house and its ground from the pottery yard and works, but only partly. Through the hedge could be seen the desolate yard, and the many-windowed, factory-like pottery, over the hedge could be seen the chimneys and the outhouses. But inside the hedge, a pleasant garden and lawn sloped down to a willow pool, which had once supplied the works.

The pottery itself was now closed, the great doors of the yard permanently shut. No more the great crates with yellow straw showing through, stood in stacks by the packing shed. No more the drays drawn by great horses rolled down the hill with a high load. No more the pottery lasses in their clay-coloured overalls, their faces and hair splashed with grey fine mud, shrieked and larked with the men. All that was over.

'We like it much better – oh, much better – quieter,' said Matilda Rockley.

'Oh, yes,' assented Emmie Rockley, her sister.

'I'm sure you do,' agreed the visitor.

But whether the two Rockley girls really liked it better, or whether they only imagined they did, is a question. Certainly their lives were much more grey and dreary now that the grey clay had ceased to spatter its mud and silt its dust over the premises. They did not quite realise how they missed the shrieking, shouting lasses, whom they had known all their lives and disliked so much.

Matilda and Emmie were already old maids. In a thorough industrial district, it is not easy for the girls who have expectations above the common to find husbands. The ugly industrial town was full of men, young men who were ready to marry. But they were all colliers or pottery-hands, mere workmen. The Rockley girls would have about ten thousand pounds each when their father died: ten thousand pounds' worth of profitable house property. It was not to be sneezed at; they felt so themselves, and refrained from sneezing away such a fortune on any mere member of the proletariat. Consequently, bank clerks or nonconformist clergymen or even schoolteachers having failed to come forward, Matilda had begun to give up all idea of ever leaving the Pottery House.

Matilda was a tall, thin, graceful fair girl, with a rather large nose. She was the Mary to Emmie's Martha, that is, Matilda loved painting and music, and read a good many novels, whilst Emmie looked after the housekeeping. Emmie was shorter, plumper than her sister, and she had no accomplishments. She looked up to Matilda, whose mind was naturally refined and sensible.

In their quiet, melancholy way, the two girls were happy. Their mother was dead. Their father was ill also. He was an intelligent man who had had some education, but preferred to remain as if he were one with the rest of the working people. He had a passion for music and played the violin pretty well. But now he was getting old, he was very ill, dying of a kidney disease. He had been rather a heavy whisky-drinker.

This quiet household, with one servant maid, lived on year after year in the Pottery House. Friends came in, the girls went out, the father drank himself more and more ill. Outside in the street there was a continual racket of the colliers and their dogs and children. But inside the pottery wall was a deserted quiet.

In all this ointment there was one little fly. Ted Rockley, the father of the girls, had had four daughters, and no son. As his girls grew, he felt angry at finding himself always in a household of women. He went off to London and adopted a boy out of a charity institution. Emmie was fourteen years old, and Matilda sixteen, when their father arrived home with his prodigy, the boy of six, Hadrian.

Hadrian was just an ordinary boy from a charity home, with ordinary brownish hair and ordinary bluish eyes and of ordinary rather cockney speech. The Rockley girls – there were three at home at the time of his arrival – had resented his being sprung on them. He, with his watchful, charity-institution instinct, knew this at once. Though he was only six years old, Hadrian had a subtle, jeering look on his face when he regarded the three young women. They insisted he should address them as Cousin: Cousin Flora, Cousin Matilda, Cousin Emmie. He complied, but there seemed a mockery in his tone.

The girls, however, were kind-hearted by nature. Flora married and left home. Hadrian did very much as he pleased with Matilda and Emmie, though they had certain strictnesses. He grew up in the Pottery House and about the pottery premises, went to an elementary school, and was invariably called Hadrian Rockley. He regarded Cousin Matilda and Cousin Emmie with a certain laconic indifference, was quiet and reticent in his ways. The girls called him sly, but that was unjust. He was merely cautious, and without frankness. His Uncle, Ted Rockley, understood him tacitly; their natures were somewhat akin. Hadrian and the elderly man had a real but unemotional regard for one another.

When he was thirteen years old the boy was sent to a high school in the county town. He did not like it. His Cousin Matilda had longed to make a little gentleman of him, but he refused to be made. He would give a little contemptuous curve to his lip, and take on a shy, charity-boy grin, when refinement was thrust upon him. He played truant from the high school, sold his books, his cap with its badge, even his very scarf and pocket handkerchief, to his school-fellows, and went raking off heaven knows where with the money. So he spent two very unsatisfactory years.

When he was fifteen he announced that he wanted to leave England and go to the colonies. He had kept touch with the home. The Rockleys knew that, when Hadrian made a declaration, in his quiet, half-jeering manner, it was worse than useless to oppose him. So at last the boy departed, going to Canada under the protection of the institution to which he had belonged. He said goodbye to the Rockleys without a word of thanks, and parted, it seemed, without a pang. Matilda and Emmie wept often to think of how he left them; even on their father's face a queer look came. But Hadrian wrote fairly regularly from Canada. He had entered some electricity works near Montreal, and was doing well.

At last, however, the war came. In his turn, Hadrian joined up and came to Europe. The Rockleys saw nothing of him. They lived on, just the same, in the Pottery House. Ted Rockley was dying of a sort of dropsy, and in his heart he wanted to see the boy. When the armistice was signed, Hadrian had a long leave, and wrote that he was coming home to the Pottery House.

The girls were terribly fluttered. To tell the truth, they were a little afraid of Hadrian. Matilda, tall and thin, was frail in her health, both girls were worn with nursing their father. To have Hadrian, a young man of twenty-one, in the house with them, after he had left them so coldly five years before, was a trying circumstance.

They were in a flutter. Emmie persuaded her father to have his bed made finally in the morning room downstairs, whilst his room upstairs was prepared for Hadrian. This was done, and preparations were going on for the arrival, when, at ten o'clock in the morning the young man suddenly turned up, quite unexpectedly. Cousin Emmie, with her hair bobbed up in absurd little bobs round her forehead, was busily polishing the stair-rods, while Cousin Matilda was in the kitchen washing the drawing-room ornaments in a lather, her sleeves rolled back on her thin arms, and her head tied up oddly and coquettishly in a duster.

Cousin Matilda blushed deep with mortification when the self-possessed young man walked in with his kitbag, and put his cap on the sewing machine. He was little and self-confident, with a curious neatness about him that still suggested the charity institution. His face was brown, he had a small moustache; he was vigorous enough in his smallness.

'*Well*, is it Hadrian!' exclaimed Cousin Matilda, wringing the lather off her hand. 'We didn't expect you till tomorrow.'

'I got off Monday night,' said Hadrian, glancing round the room.

'Fancy!' said Cousin Matilda. Then, having dried her hands, she went forward, held out her hand, and said, 'How are you?'

'Quite well, thank you,' said Hadrian.

'You're quite a man,' said Cousin Matilda.

Hadrian glanced at her. She did not look her best: so thin, so large-nosed, with that pink-and-white checked duster tied round her head. She felt her disadvantage. But she had had a good deal of suffering and sorrow, she did not mind any more.

The servant entered – one that did not know Hadrian.

'Come and see my father,' said Cousin Matilda.

In the hall they roused Cousin Emmie like a partridge from cover. She was on the stairs pushing the bright stair-rods into place. Instinctively her hand went to the little knobs, her front hair bobbed on her forehead.

'Why!' she exclaimed, crossly. 'What have you come today for?'

'I got off a day earlier,' said Hadrian, and his man's voice so deep and unexpected was like a blow to Cousin Emmie.

'Well, you've caught us in the midst of it,' she said, with resentment. Then all three went into the middle room.

Mr Rockley was dressed – that is, he had on his trousers and socks – but he was resting on the bed, propped up just under the window, from whence he could see his beloved and resplendent garden, where tulips and apple trees were ablaze. He did not look as ill as he was, for the water puffed him up, and his face kept its colour. His stomach was much swollen. He glanced round swiftly, turning his eyes without turning his head. He was the wreck of a handsome, well-built man.

Seeing Hadrian, a queer, unwilling smile went over his face. The young man greeted him sheepishly.

'You wouldn't make a lifeguardsman,' he said. 'Do you want something to eat?'

Hadrian looked round – as if for the meal.

'I don't mind,' he said.

'What shall you have – egg and bacon?' asked Emmie shortly.

'Yes, I don't mind,' said Hadrian.

The sisters went down to the kitchen, and sent the servant to finish the stairs.

'Isn't he *altered*?' said Matilda, *sotto voce*.

'Isn't he!' said Cousin Emmie. '*What* a little man!'

They both made a grimace, and laughed nervously.

'Get the frying pan,' said Emmie to Matilda.

'But he's as cocky as ever,' said Matilda, narrowing her eyes and shaking her head knowingly, as she handed the frying pan.

'Mannie!' said Emmie sarcastically. Hadrian's new-fledged, cocksure manliness evidently found no favour in her eyes.

'Oh, he's not bad,' said Matilda. 'You don't want to be prejudiced against him.'

'I'm not prejudiced against him; I think he's all right for looks,' said Emmie, 'but there's too much of the little mannie about him.'

'Fancy catching us like this,' said Matilda.

'They've no thought for anything,' said Emmie with contempt. 'You go up and get dressed, our Matilda. I don't care about him. I can see to things, and you can talk to him. I shan't.'

'He'll talk to my father,' said Matilda, meaningful.

'*Sly* –!' exclaimed Emmie, with a grimace.

The sisters believed that Hadrian had come hoping to get something out of their father – hoping for a legacy. And they were not at all sure he would not get it.

Matilda went upstairs to change. She had thought it all out how she would receive Hadrian, and impress him. And he had caught her with her head tied up in a duster, and her thin arms in a basin of lather. But she did not care. She now dressed herself most scrupulously, carefully folded her long, beautiful, blonde hair, touched her pallor with a little rouge, and put her long string of exquisite crystal beads over her soft green dress. Now she looked elegant, like a heroine in a magazine illustration, and almost as unreal.

She found Hadrian and her father talking away. The young man was short of speech as a rule, but he could find his tongue with his 'uncle'. They were both sipping a glass of brandy, and smoking, and chatting like a pair of old cronies. Hadrian was telling about Canada. He was going back there when his leave was up.

'You wouldn't like to stop in England, then?' said Mr Rockley.

'No, I wouldn't stop in England,' said Hadrian.

'How's that? There's plenty of electricians here,' said Mr Rockley.

'Yes. But there's too much difference between the men and the employers over here – too much of that for me,' said Hadrian.

The sick man looked at him narrowly, with oddly smiling eyes.

'That's it, is it?' he replied.

Matilda heard and understood. 'So that's your big idea, is it, my little man,' she said to herself. She had always said of Hadrian that he had no proper *respect* for anybody or anything, that he was sly and *common*. She went down to the kitchen for a *sotto voce* confab with Emmie.

'He thinks a rare lot of himself!' she whispered.

'He's somebody, he is!' said Emmie with contempt.

'He thinks there's too much difference between masters and men, over here,' said Matilda.

'Is it any different in Canada?' asked Emmie.

'Oh, yes – democratic,' replied Matilda, 'He thinks they're all on a level over there.'

'Ay, well he's over here now,' said Emmie dryly, 'so he can keep his place.'

As they talked they saw the young man sauntering down the garden, looking casually at the flowers. He had his hands in his pockets, and his soldier's cap neatly on his head. He looked quite at his ease, as if in possession. The two women, fluttered, watched him through the window.

'We know what he's come for,' said Emmie churlishly. Matilda looked a long time at the neat khaki figure. It had something of the charity boy about it still, but now it was a man's figure, laconic, charged with plebeian energy. She thought of the derisive passion in his voice as he had declaimed against the propertied classes to her father.

'You don't know, Emmie. Perhaps he's not come for that,' she rebuked her sister. They were both thinking of the money.

They were still watching the young soldier. He stood away at the bottom of the garden, with his back to them, his hands in his pockets, looking into the water of the willow pond. Matilda's dark blue eyes had a strange, full look in them, the lids, with the faint blue veins showing, dropped rather low. She carried her head light and high, but she had a look of pain. The young man at the bottom of the garden turned and looked up the path. Perhaps he saw them through the window. Matilda moved into shadow.

That afternoon their father seemed weak and ill. He was easily exhausted. The doctor came, and told Matilda that the sick man might die suddenly at any moment – but then he might not. They must be prepared.

So the day passed, and the next. Hadrian made himself at home. He went about in the morning in his brownish jersey and his khaki trousers, collarless, his bare neck showing. He explored the pottery premises, as if he had some secret purpose in so doing; he talked with Mr Rockley, when the sick man had strength. The two girls were always angry when the two men sat talking together like cronies. Yet it was chiefly a kind of politics they talked.

On the second day after Hadrian's arrival, Matilda sat with her father in the evening. She was drawing a picture that she wanted to copy. It was very still: Hadrian was gone out somewhere, no one knew where, and Emmie was busy. Mr Rockley reclined on his bed, looking out in silence over his evening-sunny garden.

'If anything happens to me, Matilda,' he said, 'you won't sell this house – you'll stop here –'

Matilda's eyes took their slightly haggard look as she stared at her father.

'Well, we couldn't do anything else,' she said.

'You don't know what you might do,' he said. 'Everything is left to you and Emmie, equally. You do as you like with it – only don't sell this house, don't part with it.'

'No,' she said.

'And give Hadrian my watch and chain, and a hundred pounds out of what's in the bank – and help him if he ever wants helping. I haven't put his name in the will.'

'Your watch and chain, and a hundred pounds – yes. But you'll be here when he goes back to Canada, Father.'

'You never know what'll happen,' said her father.

Matilda sat and watched him, with her full, haggard eyes, for a long time, as if tranced. She saw that he knew he must go soon – she saw like a clairvoyant.

Later on she told Emmie what her father had said about the watch and chain and the money.

'What right has *he*' – he, meaning Hadrian – 'to my father's watch and chain – what has it to do with him? Let him have the money, and get off,' said Emmie. She loved her father.

That night Matilda sat late in her room. Her heart was anxious and breaking, her mind seemed entranced. She was too much entranced even to weep, and all the time she thought of her father, only her father. At last she felt she must go to him.

It was near midnight. She went along the passage and to his room. There was a faint light from the moon outside. She listened at his door. Then she softly opened and entered. The room was faintly dark. She heard a movement on the bed.

'Are you asleep?' she said softly, advancing to the side of the bed.

'Are you asleep?' she repeated gently, as she stood at the side of the bed. And she reached her hand in the darkness to touch his forehead. Delicately, her fingers met the nose and the eyebrows; she laid her fine, delicate hand on his brow. It seemed fresh and smooth – very fresh and smooth. A sort of surprise stirred her, in her entranced state. But it could not waken her. Gently, she leaned over the bed and stirred her fingers over the low-growing hair on his brow.

'Can't you sleep tonight?' she said.

There was a quick stirring in the bed. 'Yes, I can,' a voice answered. It was Hadrian's voice. She started away. Instantly, she was wakened from her late-at-night trance. She remembered that her father was downstairs, that Hadrian had his room. She stood in the darkness as if stung.

'It is you, Hadrian?' she said. 'I thought it was my father.' She was so startled, so shocked, that she could not move. The young man gave an uncomfortable laugh, and turned in his bed.

At last she got out of the room. When she was back in her own room, in the light, and her door was closed, she stood holding up her hand that had touched him, as if it were hurt. She was almost too shocked; she could not endure.

'Well,' said her calm and weary mind, 'it was only a mistake, why take any notice of it.'

But she could not reason her feelings so easily. She suffered, feeling herself in a false position. Her right hand, which she had laid so gently on his face, on his fresh skin, ached now, as if it were really injured. She could not forgive Hadrian for the mistake: it made her dislike him deeply.

Hadrian, too, slept badly. He had been awakened by the opening of the door, and had not realised what the question meant. But the soft, straying tenderness of her hand on his face startled something out of his soul. He was a charity boy, aloof and more or less at bay. The fragile exquisiteness of her caress startled him most, revealed unknown things to him.

In the morning she could feel the consciousness in his eyes, when she came downstairs. She tried to bear herself as if nothing at all had happened, and she succeeded. She had the calm self-control, self-indifference, of one who has suffered and borne her suffering. She looked at him from her darkish, almost drugged blue eyes, she met the spark of consciousness in his eyes, and quenched it. And with her long, fine hand she put the sugar in his coffee.

But she could not control him as she thought she could. He had a keen memory stinging his mind, a new set of sensations working in his consciousness. Something new was alert in him.

At the back of his reticent, guarded mind he kept his secret alive and vivid. She was at his mercy, for he was unscrupulous, his standard was not her standard.

He looked at her curiously. She was not beautiful, her nose was too large, her chin was too small, her neck was too thin. But her skin was clear and fine, she had a high-bred sensitiveness. This queer, brave, high-bred quality she shared with her father. The charity boy could see it in her tapering fingers, which were white and ringed. The same glamour that he knew in the elderly man he now saw in the woman. And he wanted to possess himself of it, he wanted to make himself master of it. As he went about through the old pottery yard, his secretive mind schemed and worked. To be master of that strange soft delicacy such as he had felt in her hand upon his face, this was what he set himself towards. He was secretly plotting.

He watched Matilda as she went about, and she became aware of his attention, as of some shadow following her. But her pride made her ignore it. When he sauntered near her, his hands in his pockets, she received him with that same commonplace kindliness which mastered him more than any contempt. Her superior breeding seemed to control him. She made herself feel towards him exactly as she had always felt: he was a young boy who lived in the house with them, but was a stranger. Only she dared not remember his face under her hand. When she remembered that, she was bewildered. Her hand had offended her, she wanted to cut it off. And she wanted, fiercely, to cut off the memory in him. She assumed she had done so.

One day, when he sat talking with his 'uncle', he looked straight into the eyes of the sick man, and said, 'But I shouldn't like to live and die here in Rawsley.'

'No – well – you needn't,' said the sick man.

'Do you think Cousin Matilda likes it?'

'I should think so.'

'I don't call it much of a life,' said the youth. 'How much older is she than me, Uncle?'

The sick man looked at the young soldier.

'A good bit,' he said.

'Over thirty?' said Hadrian.

'Well, not so much. She's thirty-two.'

Hadrian considered a while.

'She doesn't look it,' he said.

Again the sick father looked at him.

'Do you think she'd like to leave here?' said Hadrian.

'Nay, I don't know,' replied the father, restive.

Hadrian sat still, having his own thoughts. Then in a small, quiet voice, as if he were speaking from inside himself, he said, 'I'd marry her if you wanted me to.'

The sick man raised his eyes suddenly, and stared. He stared for a long time. The youth looked inscrutably out of the window.

'*You!*' said the sick man, mocking, with some contempt. Hadrian turned and met his eyes. The two men had an inexplicable understanding.

'If you wasn't against it,' said Hadrian.

'Nay,' said the father, turning aside, 'I don't think I'm against it. I've never thought of it. But – but Emmie's the youngest.'

He had flushed, and looked suddenly more alive. Secretly he loved the boy.

'You might ask her,' said Hadrian.

The elder man considered.

'Hadn't you better ask her yourself?' he said.

'She'd take more notice of you,' said Hadrian.

They were both silent. Then Emmie came in.

For two days Mr Rockley was excited and thoughtful. Hadrian went about quietly, secretly, unquestioning. At last the father and daughter were alone together. It was very early morning; the father had been in much pain. As the pain abated, he lay still, thinking.

'Matilda!' he said suddenly, looking at his daughter.

'Yes, I'm here,' she said.

'Ay! I want you to do something –'

She rose in anticipation.

'Nay, sit still. I want you to marry Hadrian –'

She thought he was raving. She rose, bewildered and frightened.

'Nay, sit you still, sit you still. You hear what I tell you.'

'But you don't know what you're saying, Father.'

'Ay, I know well enough. I want you to marry Hadrian, I tell you.'

She was dumbfounded. He was a man of few words.

'You'll do what I tell you,' he said.

She looked at him slowly. 'What put such an idea in your mind?' she said proudly.

'He did.'

Matilda almost looked her father down, her pride was so offended. 'Why, it's disgraceful,' she said.

'Why?'

She watched him slowly. 'What do you ask me for?' she said. 'It's disgusting.'

'The lad's sound enough,' he replied, testily.

'You'd better tell him to clear out,' she said, coldly.

He turned and looked out of the window. She sat flushed and erect for a long time. At length her father turned to her, looking really malevolent.

'If you won't,' he said, 'you're a fool, and I'll make you pay for your foolishness, do you see?'

Suddenly a cold fear gripped her. She could not believe her senses. She was terrified and bewildered. She stared at her father, believing him to be delirious, or mad, or drunk. What could she do?

'I tell you,' he said. 'I'll send for Whittle tomorrow if you don't. You shall neither of you have anything of mine.'

Whittle was the solicitor. She understood her father well enough: he would send for his solicitor, and make a will leaving all his property to Hadrian. Neither she nor Emmie should have anything. It was too much. She rose and went out of the room, up to her own room, where she locked herself in.

She did not come out for some hours. At last, late at night, she confided in Emmie.

'The sliving demon, he wants the money,' said Emmie. 'My father's out of his mind.'

The thought that Hadrian merely wanted the money was another blow to Matilda. She did not love the impossible youth – but she had not yet learnt to think of him as a thing of evil. He now became hideous to her mind.

Emmie had a little scene with her father next day.

'You don't mean what you said to our Matilda yesterday, do you, Father?' she asked aggressively.

'Yes,' he replied.

'What, that you'll alter your will?'

'Yes.'

'You won't,' said his angry daughter.

But he looked at her with a malevolent little smile.

'Annie!' he shouted. 'Annie!' He had still power to make his voice carry. The servant maid came in from the kitchen. 'Put your things on, and go down to Whittle's office, and say I want to see Mr Whittle as soon as he can, and will he bring a will form.'

The sick man lay back a little – he could not lie down. His daughter sat as if she had been struck. Then she left the room.

Hadrian was pottering about in the garden. She went straight down to him.

'Here,' she said. 'You'd better get off. You'd better take your things and go from here, quick.'

Hadrian looked slowly at the infuriated girl. 'Who says so?' he asked.

'*We* say so – get off, you've done enough mischief and damage.'

'Does Uncle say so?'

'Yes, he does.'

'I'll go and ask him.'

But like a fury Emmie barred his way. 'No, you needn't. You needn't ask him nothing at all. We don't want you, so you can go.'

'Uncle's boss here.'

'A man that's dying, and you crawling round and working on him for his money! You're not fit to live.'

'Oh!' he said. 'Who says I'm working for his money?'

'I say. But my father told our Matilda, and *she* knows what you are. *She* knows what you're after. So you might as well clear out, for all you'll get – guttersnipe!'

He turned his back on her, to think. It had not occurred to him that they would think he was after the money. He *did* want the money – badly. He badly wanted to be an employer himself, not one of the employed. But he knew, in his subtle, calculating way, that it was not for money he wanted Matilda. He wanted both the money and Matilda. But he told himself the two desires were separate, not one. He could not do with Matilda, *without* the money. But he did not want her *for* the money.

When he got this clear in his mind, he sought for an opportunity to tell it her, lurking and watching. But she avoided him. In the evening the lawyer came. Mr Rockley seemed to have a new access of strength – a will was drawn up, making the previous arrangements wholly conditional. The old will held good if Matilda would consent to marry Hadrian. If she refused, then at the end of six months the whole property passed to Hadrian.

Mr Rockley told this to the young man, with malevolent satisfaction. He seemed to have a strange desire, quite unreasonable, for revenge upon the women who had surrounded him for so long, and served him so carefully.

'Tell her in front of me,' said Hadrian.

So Mr Rockley sent for his daughters.

At last they came, pale, mute, stubborn. Matilda seemed to have retired far off, Emmie seemed like a fighter ready to fight to the death. The sick man reclined on the bed, his eyes bright, his puffed hand trembling. But his face had again some of its old, bright handsomeness. Hadrian sat quiet, a little aside – the indomitable, dangerous charity boy.

'There's the will,' said their father, pointing them to the paper.

The two women sat mute and immovable, they took no notice.

'Either you marry Hadrian, or he has everything,' said the father with satisfaction.

'Then let him have everything,' said Matilda boldly.

'He's not! He's not!' cried Emmie fiercely. 'He's not going to have it. The guttersnipe!'

An amused look came on her father's face.

'You hear that, Hadrian,' he said.

'I didn't offer to marry Cousin Matilda for the money,' said Hadrian, flushing and moving on his seat.

Matilda looked at him slowly, with her dark blue, drugged eyes. He seemed a strange little monster to her.

'Why, you liar, you know you did,' cried Emmie.

The sick man laughed. Matilda continued to gaze strangely at the young man.

'She knows I didn't,' said Hadrian.

He too had his courage, as a rat has indomitable courage in the end. Hadrian had some of the neatness, the reserve, the underground quality of the rat. But he had perhaps the ultimate courage, the most unquenchable courage of all.

Emmie looked at her sister. 'Oh, well,' she said. 'Matilda – don't bother. Let him have everything, we can look after ourselves.'

'I know he'll take everything,' said Matilda, abstractedly.

Hadrian did not answer. He knew in fact that if Matilda refused him he would take everything, and go off with it.

'A clever little mannie –! ' said Emmie, with a jeering grimace.

The father laughed noiselessly to himself. But he was tired. 'Go on, then,' he said. 'Go on, let me be quiet.'

Emmie turned and looked at him. 'You deserve what you've got,' she said to her father bluntly.

'Go on,' he answered mildly. 'Go on.'

Another night passed – a night nurse sat up with Mr Rockley. Another day came. Hadrian was there as ever, in his woollen jersey and coarse khaki trousers and bare neck. Matilda went about, frail and distant, Emmie black-browed in spite of her blondness. They were all quiet, for they did not intend the mystified servant to learn anything.

Mr Rockley had very bad attacks of pain; he could not breathe. The end seemed near. They all went about quiet and stoical, all unyielding. Hadrian pondered within himself. If he did not marry Matilda he would go to Canada with twenty thousand pounds. This was itself a very satisfactory prospect. If Matilda consented he would have nothing – she would have her own money.

Emmie was the one to act. She went off in search of the solicitor and brought him with her. There was an interview, and Whittle tried to frighten the youth into withdrawal – but without avail. The clergyman and relatives were summoned – but Hadrian stared at them and took no notice. It made him angry, however.

He wanted to catch Matilda alone. Many days went by, and he was not successful: she avoided him. At last, lurking, he surprised her one day as she came to pick gooseberries, and he cut off her retreat. He came to the point at once.

'You don't want me, then?' he said, in his subtle, insinuating voice.

'I don't want to speak to you,' she said, averting her face.

'You put your hand on me, though,' he said. 'You shouldn't have done that, and then I should never have thought of it. You shouldn't have touched me.'

'If you were anything decent, you'd know that was a mistake, and forget it,' she said.

'I know it was a mistake – but I shan't forget it. If you wake a man up, he can't go to sleep again because he's told to.'

'If you had any decent feeling in you, you'd have gone away,' she replied.

'I didn't want to,' he replied.

She looked away into the distance. At last she asked, 'What do you persecute me for, if it isn't for the money? I'm old enough to be your mother. In a way I've been your mother.'

'Doesn't matter,' he said. 'You've been no mother to me. Let us marry and go out to Canada – you might as well – you've touched me.'

She was white and trembling. Suddenly she flushed with anger. 'It's so *indecent*,' she said.

'How?' he retorted. 'You touched me.'

But she walked away from him. She felt as if he had trapped her. He was angry and depressed; he felt again despised.

That same evening she went into her father's room.

'Yes,' she said suddenly. 'I'll marry him.'

Her father looked up at her. He was in pain, and very ill. 'You like him now, do you?' he said, with a faint smile.

She looked down into his face, and saw death not far off. She turned and went coldly out of the room.

The solicitor was sent for; preparations were hastily made. In all the interval Matilda did not speak to Hadrian, never answered him if he addressed her. He approached her in the morning.

'You've come round to it, then?' he said, giving her a pleasant look from his twinkling, almost kindly eyes. She looked down at him and turned aside. She looked down on him both literally and figuratively. Still he persisted, and triumphed.

Emmie raved and wept; the secret flew abroad. But Matilda was silent and unmoved, Hadrian was quiet and satisfied, and nipped with fear also. But he held out against his fear. Mr Rockley was very ill, but unchanged.

On the third day the marriage took place. Matilda and Hadrian drove straight home from the registrar, and went straight into the room of the dying man. His face lit up with a clear twinkling smile.

'Hadrian – you've got her?' he said, a little hoarsely.

'Yes,' said Hadrian, who was pale round the gills.

'Ay, my lad, I'm glad you're mine,' replied the dying man. Then he turned his eyes closely on Matilda.

'Let's look at you, Matilda,' he said. Then his voice went strange and unrecognisable. 'Kiss me,' he said.

She stooped and kissed him. She had never kissed him before, not since she was a tiny child. But she was quiet, very still.

'Kiss him,' the dying man said.

Obediently, Matilda put forward her mouth and kissed the young husband.

'That's right! That's right!' murmured the dying man.